W9-DIV-402

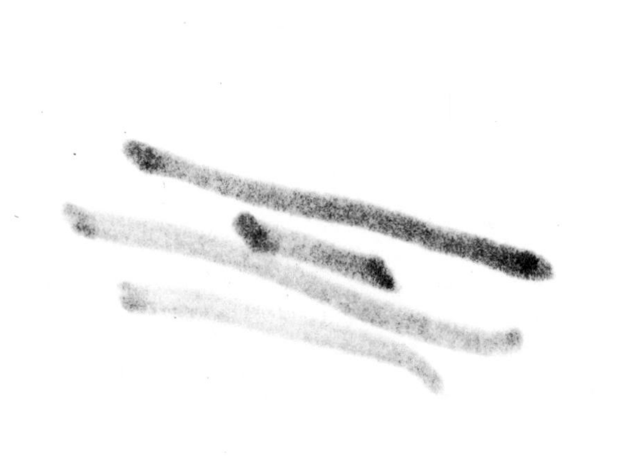

Observing the Universe

Secrets of the Universe

Giles Sparrow

WORLD ALMANAC® LIBRARY

Please visit our web site at: www.garethstevens.com
For a free color catalog describing World Almanac® Library's list of high-quality books and multimedia programs, call 1-800-848-2928 (USA) or 1-800-387-3178 (Canada). World Almanac® Library's fax: (414) 332-3567.

Library of Congress Cataloging-in-Publication Data

Sparrow, Giles.
Observing the universe / by Giles Sparrow.
p. cm. — (Secrets of the universe)
Includes bibliographical references and index.
ISBN-10: 0-8368-7277-0 — ISBN-13: 978-0-8368-7277-4 (lib. bdg.)
ISBN-10: 0-8368-7284-3 — ISBN-13: 978-0-8368-7284-2 (softcover)
1. Astronomy—Juvenile literature. 2. Telescopes—Juvenile literature.
I. Title. II. Series: Sparrow, Giles. Secrets of the universe. III. Series.
QB46.S696 2007
520—dc22 2006009957

This North American edition first published in 2007 by
World Almanac® Library
A Member of the WRC Media Family of Companies
330 West Olive Street, Suite 100
Milwaukee, WI 53212 USA

Amber Books project editor: James Bennett
Amber Books design: Richard Mason
Amber Books picture research: Terry Forshaw

World Almanac® Library editor: Carol Ryback
World Almanac® Library designer: Scott M. Krall
World Almanac® Library art direction: Tammy West
World Almanac® Library production: Jessica Morris and Robert L. Kraus

Picture acknowledgments: 42 (Jim Sugar). Getty Images: 6 (National Geographic/Richard T. Nowitz); 7, 11 (Stock Montage); 14 (Eric Bean); 40 (Wayne Levin); 41 (Time & Life Pictures); 43 (Al Fenn). Popperfoto: 9, 10 (left). R. Sheridan/Ancient Art & Architecture Collection: 4. Topfoto: 10 (right.) All artworks courtesy of International Masters Publishers Ltd.

Printed in the United States of America

1 2 3 4 5 6 7 8 9 10 09 08 07 06

CONTENTS

THE HISTORY OF ASTRONOMY 4

OPTICAL OBSERVATION 14

OBSERVING THE SOLAR SYSTEM 22

OBSERVING THE STARS 30

SUPER ASTRONOMY 38

GLOSSARY 46

FURTHER INFORMATION 47

INDEX 48

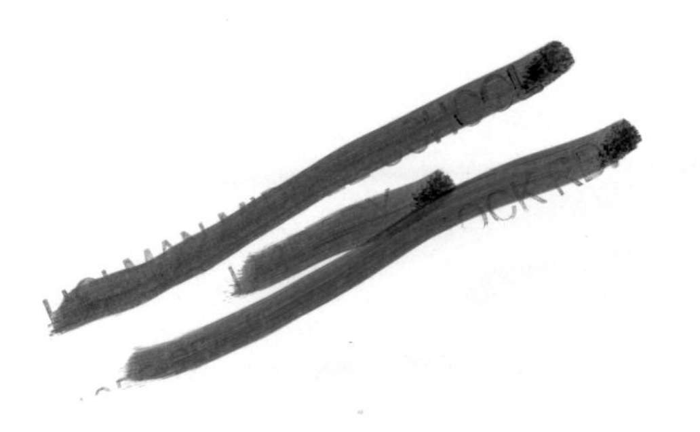

Cover and title page: Mountaintops that reach above the clouds into the thinner portions of the atmosphere make the best locations for observing outer space from Earth. Space-based telescopes that operate on a variety of electromagnetic wavelengths provide even more data about the universe.

CHAPTER 1

THE HISTORY OF ASTRONOMY

Astronomy is the oldest, and possibly the most fascinating, science. Long before recorded history, people have marveled at the sky and attempted to explain the heavens. New theories constantly arrived and replaced old ideas, so astronomers have continually revised their vision of our place in the cosmos.

Ancient stargazers

Astronomy began before writing and left its traces behind in some of the world's ancient monuments. In about 3000 B.C., the people of northern Europe built huge stone rows and circles such as Stonehenge pointed toward the rising and setting points of the Sun and Moon during certain times of the year. A few centuries later, when the ancient Egyptians built the Great Pyramid at Giza, they drove a shaft extending through one of the walls deep into the interior where the pharaoh was entombed. This shaft aligned with a constellation so that the pharaoh could look directly up at the star formation from where he was laid to rest. The Egyptians believed this would help the pharaoh make his journey into the afterlife. Other ancient temples, found in countries in Southeast Asia and Central America, were also deliberately built to align with the rising and setting points of various astronomical objects.

By the time of the first written records, the ancient astronomers were already very knowledgeable. The Egyptians, for example, predicted the Nile River's flood season from the position of the bright star Sirius before sunrise. The Babylonians could predicted the movements of the planets. Stonehenge probably helped predict eclipses. In every culture that left records, we find that objects in the sky were associated with gods and mythical creatures. Astrology—the idea that the stars and planets could influence events on Earth—was born from those beliefs.

Built in about the first century B.C. at Dendera in Egypt, the Temple of Hathor boasts a spectacular carved ceiling representing the Egyptian version of the zodiac.

The first theories that really attempted to explain the sky started developing in about 400 B.C. in classical Greece, where science and philosophy originated. While many of these ideas seem absurd to us now, they represented solid attempts to explain the objects and events seen in the skies. Greek and Greek-influenced thinkers were the first to measure the diameter of Earth as well as the distances to the Moon and the Sun. The Greeks were also the first to develop models that described the entire universe without resorting to storytelling and mythology for explanation.

A Greek-Egyptian astronomer living in the second century A.D. named Claudius Ptolemy (also known as Ptolemaeus) developed the most successful of these models. His theory put Earth at the center of the universe, with the Sun, the Moon, and the planets moving around it on transparent spheres, with the stars attached to the outermost sphere. In order to explain why the planets sometimes moved as if they were not in circular orbits, he gave each one a series of complex circular suborbits or "epicycles."

Stonehenge, in southwest England, is thought to be an ancient observatory and calendar. Archaeological discoveries suggest its builders were skilled astronomers who used it to predict eclipses.

Not everyone agreed that the universe was centered around Earth. As early as 300 B.C., Aristarchus of Samos suggested that Earth and the other planets might actually be moving around the Sun. Aristarchus experienced the same problems explaining his theory as Ptolemy had when explaining the movement of the planets, so Ptolemy's model became accepted as fact throughout the Roman Empire. It passed from there into the Christian church, and was accepted without question through Europe's Dark Ages (476–1000 A.D.) and for a further four hundred years into the Middle Ages, between the fifth to the fifteenth centuries.

The Copernican Revolution

Throughout the Middle Ages, European learning and culture generally looked backward, relying on the ideas of the classical world—often transmitted and garbled through the church—as the ultimate authority. Across the Muslim world, meanwhile, science was comparatively thriving. Arab astronomers developed a variety of new measuring instruments, including the astrolabe, which helped measure the movements of the planets more precisely. Starting in the eleventh century, Greek texts began to filter back into Europe (often in Arabic translations). This produced a new spirit of questioning and creativity that eventually led to the Renaissance (1350–1650 A.D.), a time when science and the arts flourished freely again.

Astronomy was also swept up in this new spirit of revival. In 1543, the last year of his life, Polish Roman Catholic priest and astronomer Nicolaus Copernicus (1473–1543) published a book suggesting again that the Sun was the center of the universe. The idea was highly controversial, and came at the same time as a religious Reformation that was splitting the Roman Catholic Church. Copernicus waited until he was on his deathbed before publishing his work. Interest in the idea spread rapidly, but the problem of the circular orbits not matching the movement of the planets remained unresolved.

The real change occurred a few years later, in about 1609. The first blow came from German

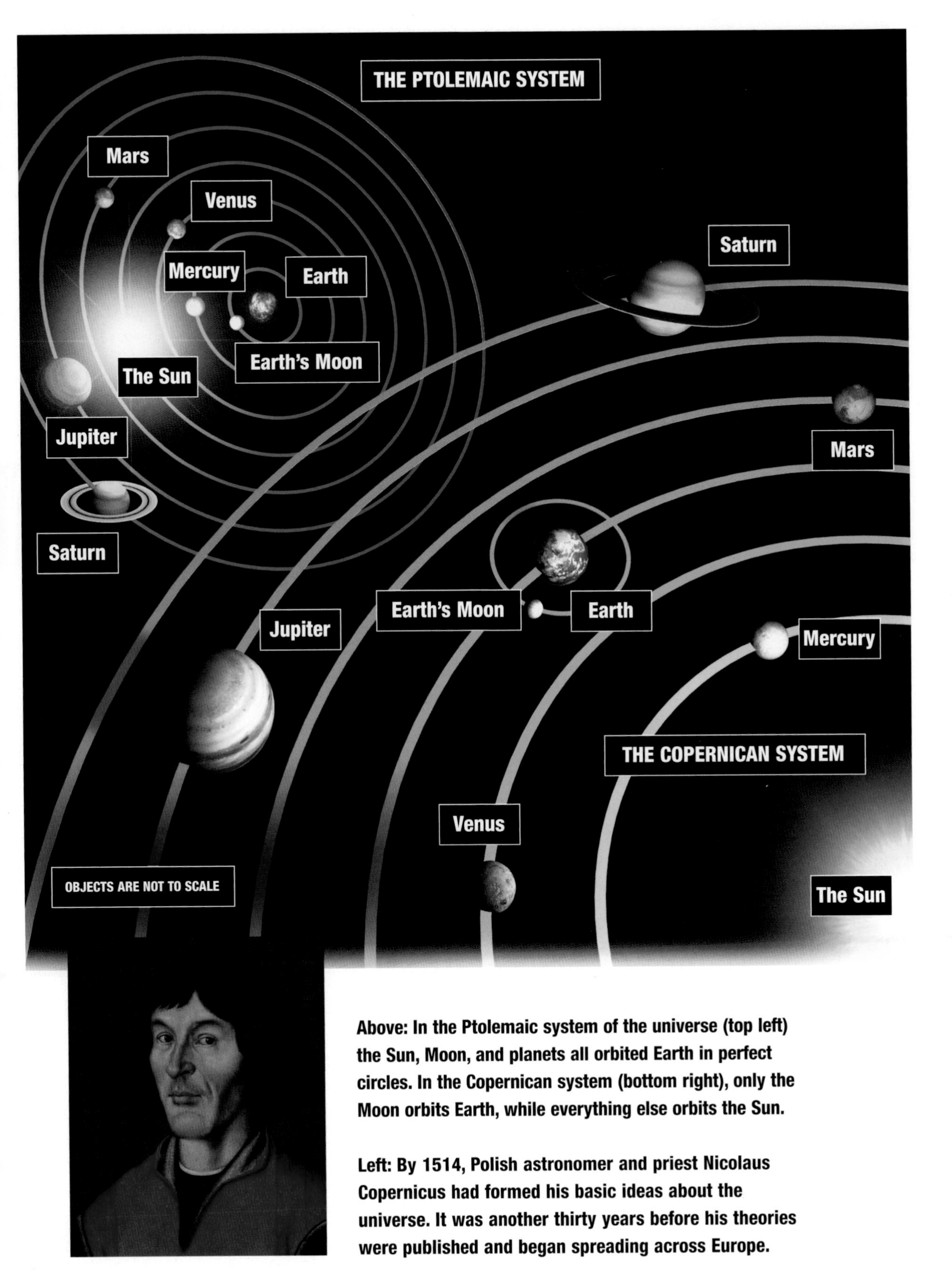

Above: In the Ptolemaic system of the universe (top left) the Sun, Moon, and planets all orbited Earth in perfect circles. In the Copernican system (bottom right), only the Moon orbits Earth, while everything else orbits the Sun.

Left: By 1514, Polish astronomer and priest Nicolaus Copernicus had formed his basic ideas about the universe. It was another thirty years before his theories were published and began spreading across Europe.

THE ELECTROMAGNETIC SPECTRUM

Light that we see is only a small part of the electromagnetic (EM) spectrum—the mostly invisible radiation, or energy, given off by stars. Electromagnetic radiation takes the form of different wavelengths of energy as it travels across the universe. All wavelengths of the EM spectrum move at the same speed: the speed of light—186,000 miles (300,000 kilometers) per second.

The visible part of the EM spectrum, in the middle, ranges from red light with longer wavelengths, to violet light with shorter wavelengths. Beyond the visible violet light, the wavelengths become increasingly short, high-energy wavelengths that give off dangerous ionizing, or "hot," radiation such as ultraviolet rays, X-rays, and gamma rays. Likewise, the wavelengths beyond red light become increasingly long, with lower energy levels, such as infrared (heat) waves, microwaves, radar waves, and radio waves.

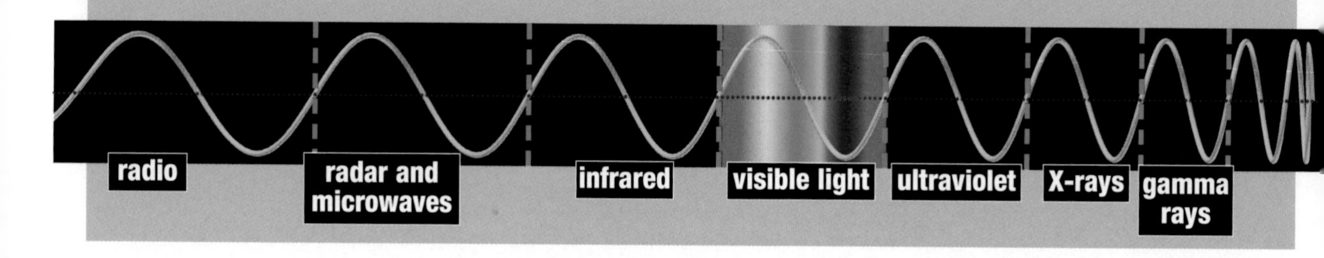

astrologer Johannes Kepler (1571–1630), who had spent years observing with the great Danish astronomer Tycho Brahe (1546–1601), using the most accurate instruments available at the time. Kepler concluded that Copernicus was right, but that the planets did not move around the Sun in exactly perfect circles. Instead, they followed stretched, elliptical (oval) paths, speeding up when closest to the Sun and slowing down when farthest away from it. Kepler's discovery coincided with the invention of the telescope (probably originating in Holland for use in warfare—not to observe the sky) and its rapid spread across Europe. Italian scientist Galileo Galilei (1564–1642) was one of the first people to study the sky with a telescope, and he discovered many features that challenged accepted ideas about the universe.

The age of the telescope

The first telescopes were primitive instruments that used small lenses to collect light and magnify images, but they were still a major improvement on the human eye. Within a few years, astronomers were able to discover the moonlike phases of Venus and Mercury, dark spots on the Sun, the host of stars in the Milky Way, and a huge wealth of features on the Moon. But this was just the beginning. Over the next two centuries, telescopes got bigger, better, and larger, leading to yet more revolutionary discoveries. Among the telescopic pioneers was Dutchman Christiaan Huygens (1629–1692), who built the largest lens telescopes of his time. He was the first person to correctly describe the rings around Saturn, and he discovered Saturn's largest moon, Titan. He also invented an eyepiece with a built-in measuring device, allowing the positions of stars to be measured with much greater accuracy.

In the 1660s, two Englishmen, philosopher and mathematician Sir Isaac Newton (1642–1726) and astronomer and mathematician James Gregory (1638–1675) independently invented reflecting telescopes, which used curved mirrors

GALILEO

Galileo Galilei was a professor of mathematics at the University of Pisa in Italy, where he began making telescopes in 1609. He discovered the four large "Galilean" moons of Jupiter, the phases of Venus, features on the Moon, and the countless stars of the Milky Way. In 1610, he published his observations in a book entitled *The Starry Messenger.* Galileo was convinced that Copernicus was right, but this led him into conflict with the authorities in the Roman Catholic Church. At the time, much of northern Europe was protesting and splitting from the Roman Catholic Church. In response, the Church set up a court called the Inquisition to investigate ideas they thought were heretical (in other words, ideas that went against their teachings). Eventually, in 1632, Galileo was called before the court for teaching the ideas of Copernicus. He refused to deny his beliefs, and as a result spent the last years of his life in jail.

A page from Galileo's notebooks records his observations of the moons of Jupiter in 1609–1610. He correctly interpreted these moving points of light as satellites in orbit around the planet, putting an end to the idea of an Earth-centered universe once and for all.

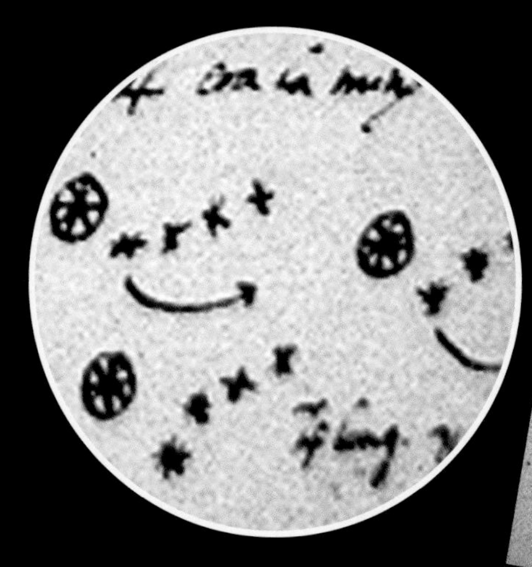

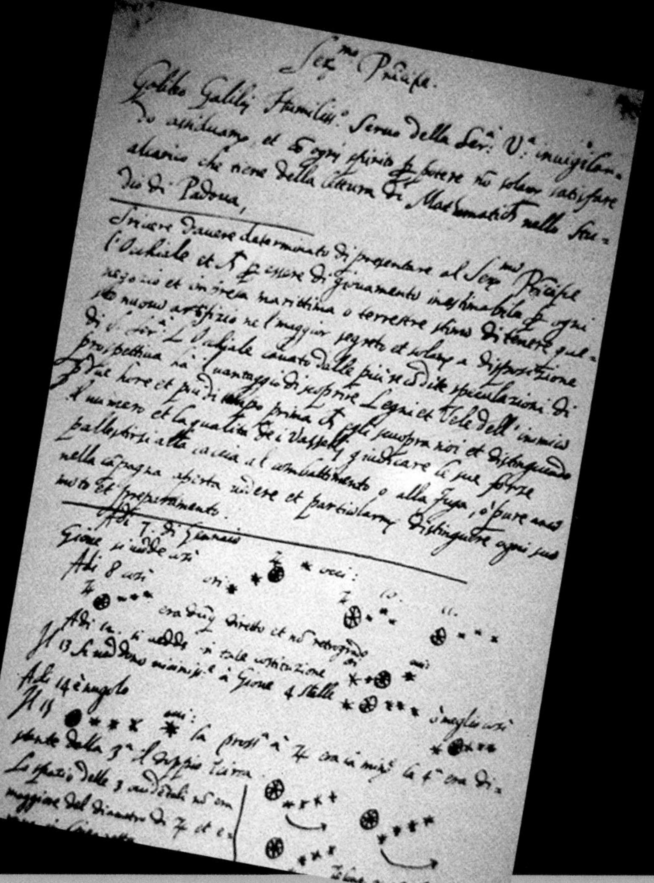

rather than glass lenses to capture and focus light. Mirrors had many advantages. They could be made more easily than lenses, and they did not absorb any of the light passing through them. Although not an astronomer himself, Newton worked closely with English astronomer Edmund Halley (1656–1742), who famously realized that a certain comet, later named after him, orbits the Sun every seventy-six years. Newton's greatest achievement was the discovery of the laws of motion and gravitation. Newton's laws helped explain Kepler's observations of how the planets could orbit the Sun.

Sir Isaac Newton (far left) invented one of the first reflecting telescopes (left). Newton mounted the eyepiece on the side of the telescope.

Many national observatories were set up during this era. The research of astronomers was badly needed at this time because the increase in trade brought the need for better navigation using the stars. By the middle of the 1700s, when the first accurate shipboard clocks were invented, navigators no longer needed to follow the stars to find their way, and relied less and less on astronomy.

The next great astronomical discoveries came at the end of the 1700s, when German-born British astronomer Sir William Herschel

OBSERVING ACROSS THE SPECTRUM

Only a small fraction of electromagnetic (EM) radiation from space reaches the surface of Earth. Although our planet's atmosphere absorbs most of the ultraviolet (UV) and some of the infrared (IR) and radio wavelengths, the visible portion of the EM spectrum makes it to the ground intact. We feel the IR radiation that penetrates the atmosphere as the Sun's heat on our bodies and other objects, while the UV rays that get through often produce skin damage, including tanning or sunburn. Still, the atmosphere also protects us from the more dangerous and damaging EM wavelengths, including X-rays and gamma rays.

We use the different wavelengths of the EM spectrum to explore space. Most ground-based telescopes scan the universe using visible light. For the clearest views, they are often located on mountaintops, where Earth's atmosphere is thinnest. On these mountain peaks, special IR telescopes also detect some of the IR radiation before the denser parts of our atmosphere block it. The best IR observing occurs from space-based telescopes, not only because of the lack of atmospheric blocking, but also because of the lack of ambient heat generated by Earth and by the IR telescope itself—which can distort images. The cold temperatures of space also require less refrigerant for cooling an orbiting IR telescope.

Earth-based radio telescopes, like the famous one in Arecibo, Puerto Rico, consist of huge metal dishes that collect

(1738–1822) discovered a new planet, Uranus, in 1781. Inspired by this discovery, many astronomers started to look for a "missing" planet between Mars and Jupiter. This led to the discovery of the first asteroids in the early 1800s. Closer studies of the orbit of Uranus helped astronomers discover Neptune—the first planet to be predicted mathematically—in 1846.

When Sir William Herschel (above, right) first saw Uranus (above), he thought he had found a comet. The new planet remained mysterious for two centuries, until *Voyager 2* photographed it in 1986.

The age of astrophysics

The early 1800s also saw the birth of a new science, known as astrophysics, as the stars finally began to give up their secrets. In 1838, German astronomer Friedrich Bessel (1784–1846) became the first person to measure the distance to a star. This naturally led to an understanding of the true brightness of the stars: They were clearly all suns in their own right.

German astronomer and optician Joseph von Fraunhofer (1787–1826) discovered dark "absorption lines" in the spectrum of the Sun in 1821. His discovery led to the development of spectroscopy (*see box, page 12*). The invention of photography in the mid-1800s allowed astronomers to capture, study, and measure light from the stars. Astronomers at the Harvard College of Observatory in Cambridge, Massachusetts, began compiling the Henry

long-wavelength radio waves from space. Smaller versions of radio telescopes, often built in movable groups called arrays, allow astronomers to combine many separate radio images into one larger image. Additionally, space-based radio telescopes collect and beam such data to Earth.

Space-based telescopes capable of studying the universe in different wavelengths became a reality in the decades after the launch of *Sputnik,* the world's first artificial satellite. While the famous *Hubble Space Telescope (HST)* collects images in visible light, it also carries equipment that scans the universe in IR—as does the *Spitzer Space Telescope (Spitzer).* Space-based UV instruments include the *Hopkins Ultraviolet Telescope,* used by space shuttle astronauts, the *Cosmic Hot Interstellar Plasma Spectrometer (CHIPS),* and the *Far Ultraviolet Spectroscopic Explorer (FUSE)* Mission. The *Wilkinson Microwave Anisotropy Probe (WMAP)* studies and maps the background microwave radiation of the universe. Space-based X-ray detectors include the *Rossi X-ray Timing Explorer* Mission, and the *XMM-Newton* and *Chandra* X-ray observatories, while the *High Energy Transient Explorer-2 (HETE-2)* Mission and *International Gamma-Ray Astrophysics Laboratory (INTEGRAL)* detect gamma-ray wavelengths. Telescopes dedicated to short-wavelength EM radiation are built to prevent these high-energy rays from simply passing right through them.

SPECTROSCOPY AND DOPPLER LIGHT SHIFTS

Spectroscopy is a special science that involves the study of the different wavelengths in the electromagnetic spectrum. Every light source, such as a star, produces a "signature" pattern of visible wavelengths and absorption lines. The absorption lines interrupt the normal spectrum pattern, indicating that certain elements contained within the light source itself are absorbing that particular wavelength. Special instruments measure and record these spectral data.

In 1842, Austrian physicist Christian Johann Doppler (1803–1853) explained why sound changes pitch as the source, observers, or medium through which the sound occurs moves or changes. (Today, we notice this "Dopple effect" most often as a fire truck's siren passes.) This Doppler effect, as it is known, also influences wavelengths of light in a similar way. Light waves coming from a star moving toward us are compressed and so look bluer. If the star is moving away from us, the light waves are stretched and appear redder. These changes of color, called Doppler shifts, allowed astronomers to measure the motion of many stars for the first time.

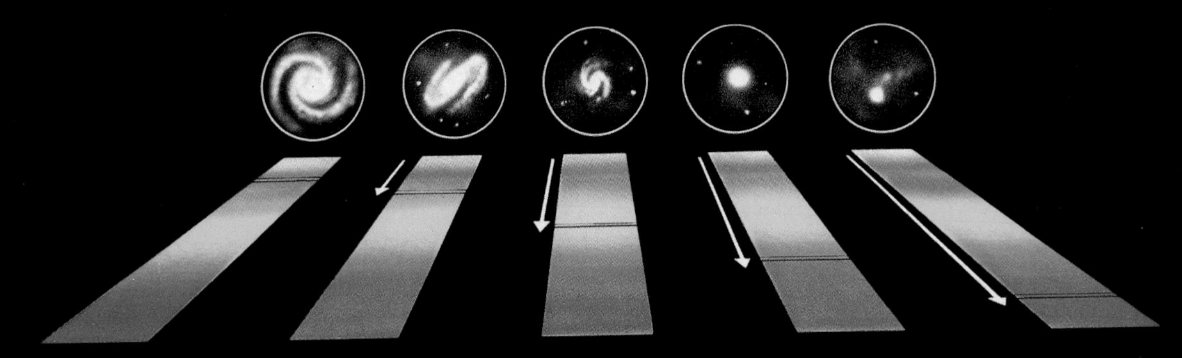

Left to right: Dark lines appear in the spectrum of light from a star or galaxy where the light has been absorbed by atoms of particular elements. As the star or galaxy moves farther away, the lines are shifted further toward the red end of the spectrum. This allows astronomers to calculate how fast stars are moving. The arrows indicate the amount of redshift in the spectrum as the galaxy recedes.

Draper catalog, which was the first detailed analysis of spectrum of the stars, around the turn of the nineteenth century.

In 1906, Danish astronomer Ejnar Hertzsprung (1873–1967) drew the first charts comparing the true brightnesses of stars with their color or "spectral type," but his work was not publicized until U.S. astronomer Henry Norris Russell (1877–1957) had the same idea seven years later. The Hertzsprung-Russell diagram reveals many important relationships between types of stars. English astronomer Sir Arthur Eddington (1882–1944) finally determined how the different areas of the chart fit together.

Eddington was also the first to suggest that the Sun might be powered by nuclear reactions in its core, though it took many years for astronomers and physicists to figure out the details. At the same time, advances in our understanding of subatomic particles led to the discovery of new and exotic types of stars, and the revival of the idea of black holes—first suggested in the 1700s.

The age of cosmology

In 1785, William Herschel devised the first map of the universe based on the distribution of stars in the sky, but during the 1800s, evidence mounted that the cosmos might contain more than just the Milky Way. Clearly, some of the fuzzy "nebulae" in the sky consisted of countless stars, but no one knew if they were small objects orbiting the Milky Way, or distant galaxies.

American Edwin Hubble (1889–1953) solved the debate in the 1920s when he measured the distance of galaxies and found that they were millions of light-years away. Hubble also made an even more important discovery: The spectral lines of many galaxies often shifted toward the red end of the spectrum, and most astronomers agreed that the galaxies moving away from Earth caused this effect. Hubble showed that the farther away a galaxy lies, the faster it is retreating. In other words, the entire universe is expanding.

If this expansion is followed back in time, it means that everything in the universe started out in one place. This was the origin of the "big bang" theory. Belgian physicist Georges Lemaître (1894–1966) first suggested the big bang theory in 1933. Russian-born U.S. physicist George Gamov (1904–1968) finally explained the physics of the big bang in the 1950s. Most importantly, Gamov predicted that the universe would still be glowing with faint radiation left over from the explosion. When this "cosmic background radiation" was discovered in 1965, most astronomers agreed that the big bang theory was correct.

Modern cosmology (the name for the study and explanation of the nature of the universe) still faces many challenges, though. We now have a good idea of the age of the universe and its current rate of expansion. Recent discoveries suggest that the expansion is actually getting faster, driven by a mysterious and unexplained force called "dark energy."

There is also a question over how much matter the universe contains. Cosmologists believe that more than 90 percent of the universe's mass could be in the form of invisible and undetectable dark matter, but they are still trying to discover the real nature of such matter.

THE SPEED OF LIGHT

All electromagnetic (EM) radiation travels through the vacuum of space at exactly the same speed—186,000 miles (300,000 km) per second. Most often, we call this the speed of light. (What we call "light" is the visible portion of the radiation of different wavelengths that make up the EM spectrum.)

In his 1905 Special Theory of Relativity, Einstein's famous equation mathematically proved that nothing could travel faster than the speed of light. For this reason, we use the speed of light as a "constant"—a unit that never changes. One light-year is the distance light travels in one Earth year, which is roughly 6 trillion miles (10 trillion km). It is a convenient way of measuring the huge distances in space. In other words, a light-year measures distances, not time.

CHAPTER 2

OPTICAL OBSERVATION

We get all our information about the universe from radiation of different wavelengths called the electromagnetic (EM) spectrum. Visible light makes up a small part of his spectrum. Until the middle of the twentieth century, astronomers could only study the sky using visible light. We study other EM wavelengths from space with special detectors that are often located above Earth's atmosphere (*see pages 39–41*). Although the unaided human eye can see many objects in the night sky, optical instruments, such as binoculars and telescopes, boost the eye's power, allowing us to see a greater range of objects and their details.

Limits of the naked eye

Human eyesight varies from person to person, but, in a remote area, most people can see between 5,000 and 6,000 stars in the dark night sky of with the naked eye. The brightness of stars is measured using a system called apparent magnitude, which originated in ancient Greece. For some reason, they set it up in a way that seems backward to us: The higher the number of magnitude, the fainter the star. The brightest stars are first magnitude, and the faintest "naked-eye" stars are sixth magnitude. When astronomers developed instruments to measure the brightness of stars directly, they standardized the system. Magnitude 6.0 marks the outer limit of faintness for naked-eye vision. Some of the brightest objects have negative magnitudes. For example, Sirius, the brightest star in the sky, has a magnitude of -1.4. Most people can see dim stars between magnitudes of 5.5 and 6.0. The most-distant object we can see with the naked eye is the Andromeda Galaxy. This gigantic spiral of stars, similar to the Milky Way, lies some 2.5 million light-years away.

Binoculars are ideal for beginners to use for observing the night sky. They brighten the image of faint objects, magnify small ones, and are fairly inexpensive.

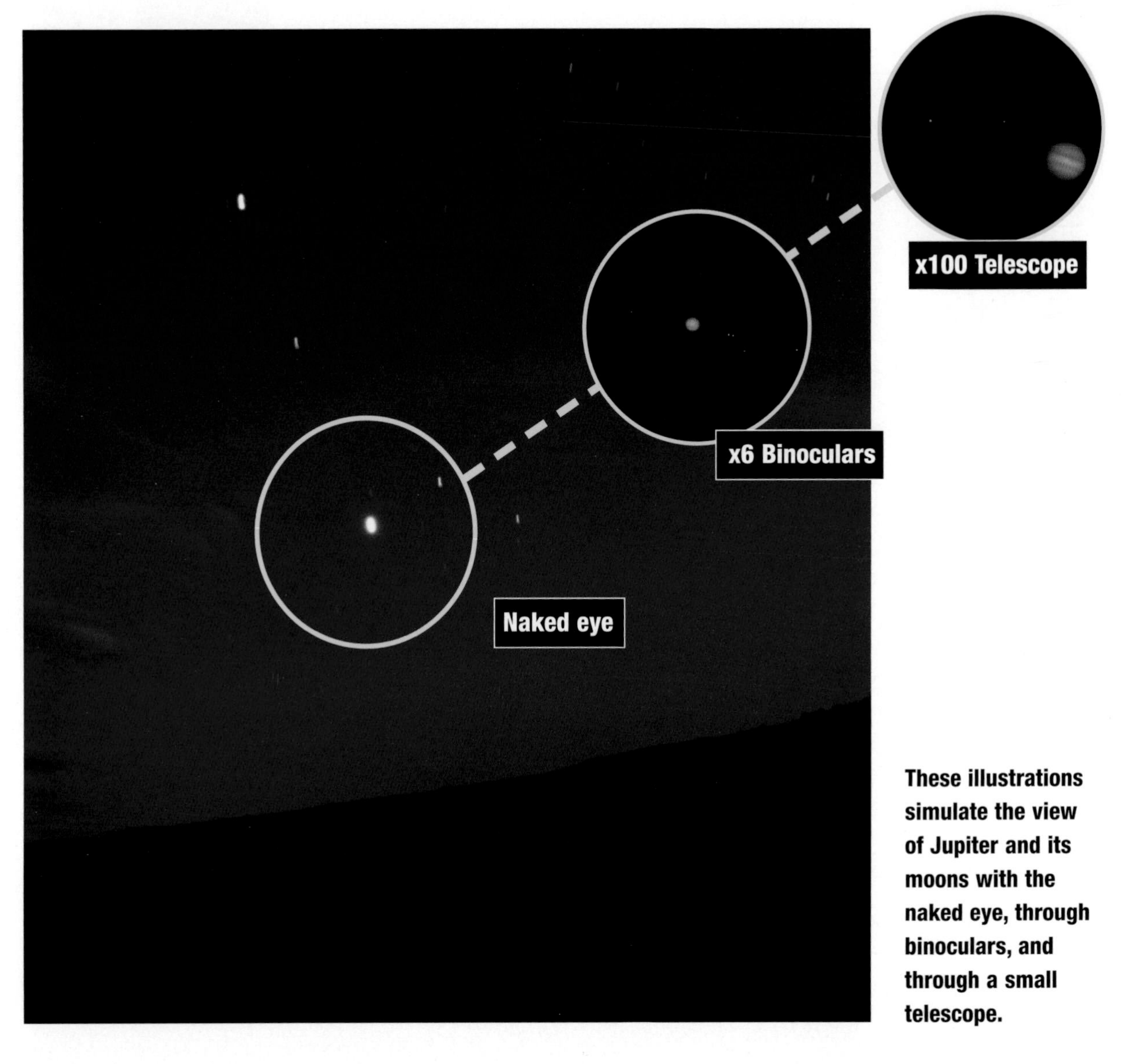

These illustrations simulate the view of Jupiter and its moons with the naked eye, through binoculars, and through a small telescope.

Optical aids

While binoculars and telescopes both boost natural eyesight, their most obvious effect is magnification. They create a "virtual image," which appears much closer to our eyes than the original object, allowing us to perceive more detail. But they also do something else that is vital for astronomy—they boost the eye's "light grasp." Because the lens or mirror of an instrument is much larger than the pupil of our eye, it collects light from a much larger area. Every celestial object produces a limited amount of light. The farther the light travels from the object, the more it spreads. So, the more starlight we can collect, the brighter the image we can produce. When this light is brought to a focus and projected into the human eye, objects that were previously invisible are made bright enough for us to see.

Any optical instrument involves two main elements. The first is a large mirror or lens—the "objective"—which collects as much light as possible and bends it toward a focus. The light rays from nearby objects are still spreading out, so a lens or mirror of a certain curvature brings rays from different distances to a focus at different points and produces a blurred image.

Fortunately, light rays from celestial objects enter the objective in a virtually parallel arrangement and come to a focus in one place: the "focal point." A telescope's second, smaller lens, the eyepiece, intercepts the light as it spreads out from the focual point and creates a "virtual image" of the object being viewed. The magnification power of a telescope depends on the combination of its lenses and mirrors.

Both the objective and the eyepiece consist of several elements. Other mirrors or prisms inserted into the telescope can divert the path of the light for specific uses.

The parts of a typical refracting telescope on an equatorial mount. Light enters through the objective lens at the front, comes to a focus, and is used to create a magnified image at the eyepiece.

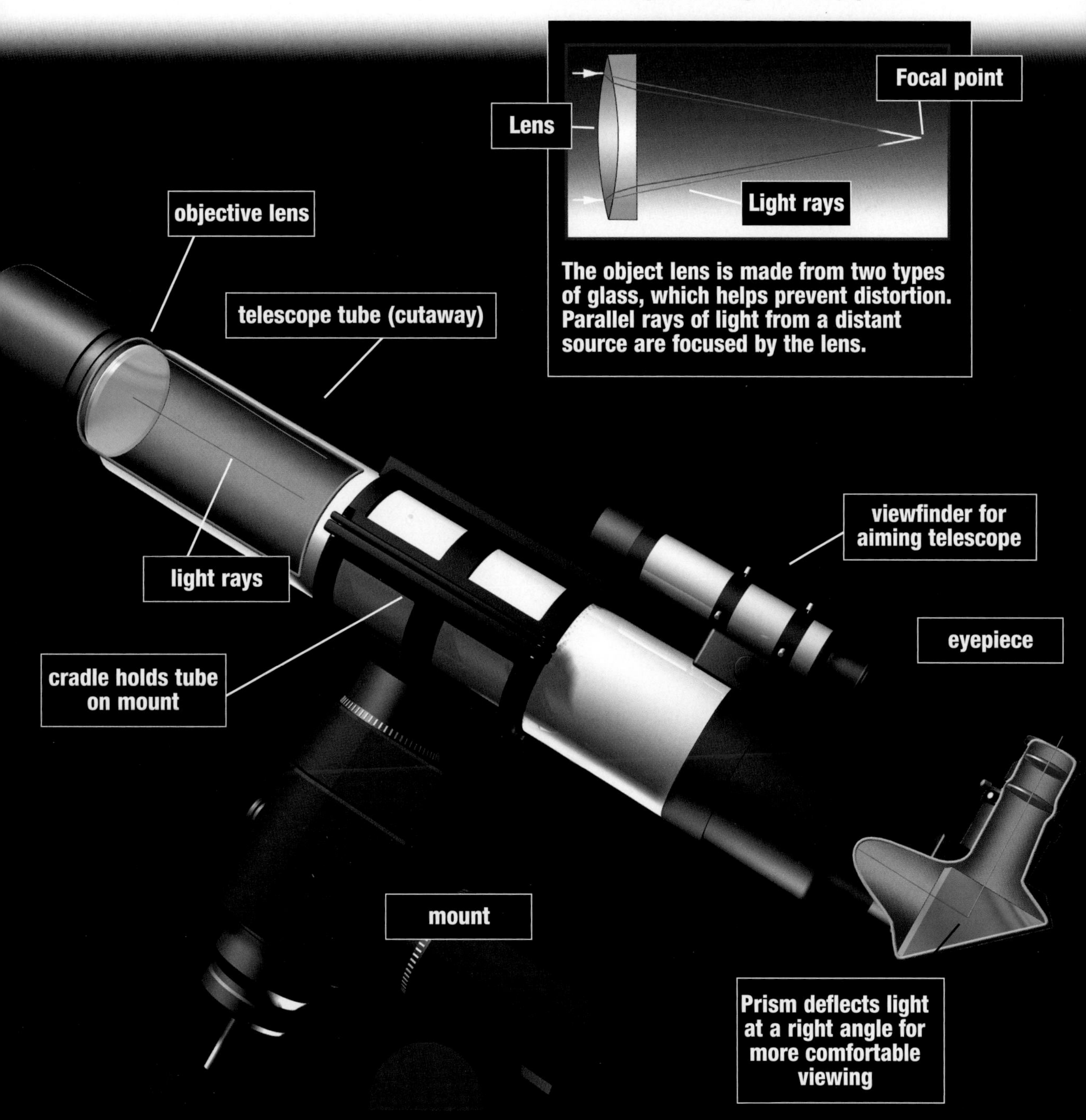

CELESTIAL COORDINATES

Astronomers need coordinates to locate objects in the sky. The simplest coordinate system is known as the alt-azimuth system. An object's altitude is its angle in degrees above the horizon. A star on the horizon has an altitude of 0 degrees, while one directly overhead (called the zenith) has an altitude of 90 degrees. Azimuth is the angle between the object and due north, measured clockwise around the horizon. The problem with this system is that the altitude and azimuth of objects changes constantly as Earth rotates, and these coordinates also depend on the observer's position on Earth.

Equatorial coordinates are more complicated to use, but they are the same for everyone, regardless of location or time. This system is based on the idea of a celestial sphere—an imaginary shell around Earth, with an axis of rotation running through Earth's poles and a celestial equator running parallel to and above Earth's equator. As Earth spins, the sphere seems to rotate once a day (although of course it is the observer who is moving). The position of a star on the celestial sphere is given by two coordinates. The first, known as declination (dec.), is its angle north or south of the celestial equator, similar to latitude on Earth. The second coordinate, known as right ascension (R.A.), is similar to longitude on Earth. Right ascension is measured counterclockwise from the point where the path of the Sun crosses the celestial equator. It is measured in hours, minutes, and seconds. There are 24 hours of R.A. all the way around the sky, just as there are 360 degrees around Earth.

THE CELESTIAL SPHERE

The red arrows show how, as Earth rotates once every day, the celestial sphere appears to spin in the opposite direction.

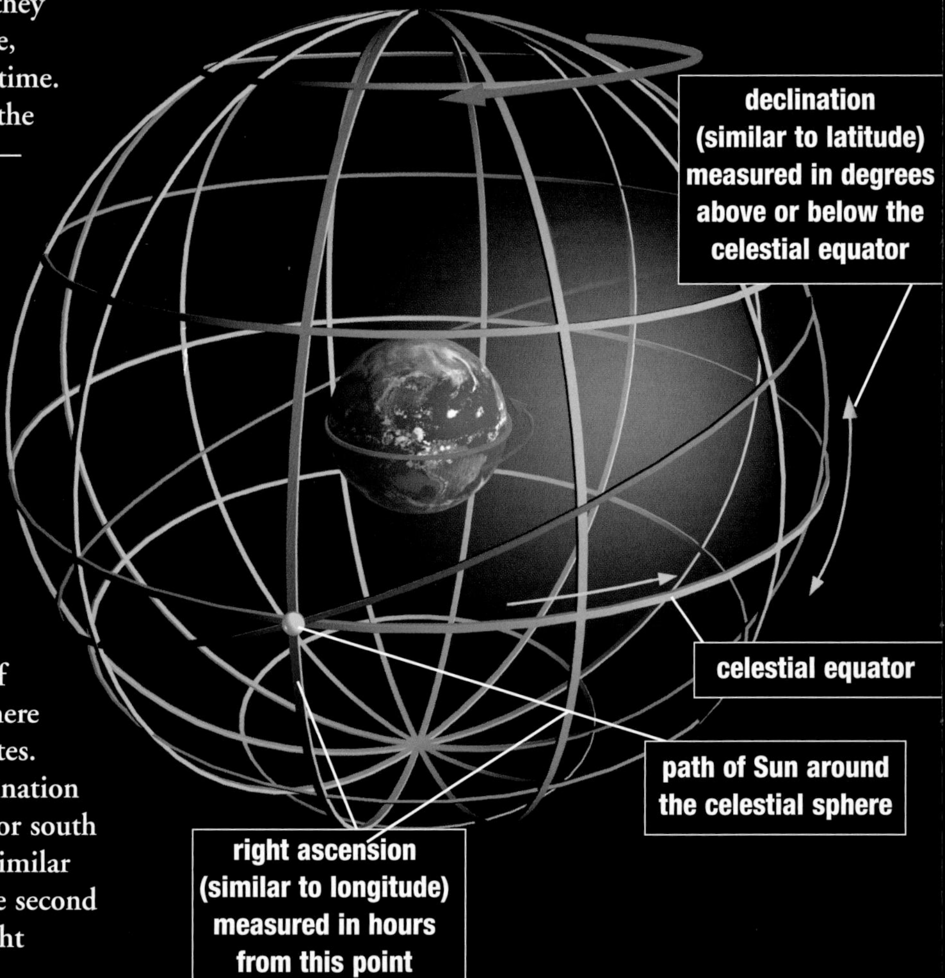

RECORDING IMAGES

It's easy to make a permanent record of the image through a telescope by replacing the eyepiece with a camera. Traditionally, images were recorded on photographic film, but today most astronomers use light-sensitive electronic wafers called Charged Coupled Devices (CCDs). This is the same kind of technology found in digital cameras. CCDs respond more rapidly to light than film and can record the exact number of rays striking each of their light-sensitive pixels. This makes them useful for photometry, the technique of measuring precise light levels in order to learn about objects. For example, computers can determine the shape of a tumbling asteroid from its changing brightnesses. Data from a number of CCD exposures can also be combined to produce a more detailed image. This is something that is impossible with traditional film.

A CCD attached to a telescope using an adapter produces detailed images.

COMPUTER-AIDED ASTRONOMY

The arrival of relatively inexpensive computing power has revolutionized amateur astronomy. The use of computer-controlled telescopes is now widespread. Once properly calibrated to the observer's position on Earth, they are able to move the telescope in both altitude and azimuth to follow an object's movement through the sky. Many come equipped with hand-held controllers that direct the telescope toward thousands of preset objects, or they can link to computers running planetarium software.

Planetarium programs can also allow people to explore the sky in detail without a telescope. Most programs contain data about hundreds of thousands of stars as well as images of planets, nebulae, and star clusters. They can generate precise images of the sky from any place on Earth, at any time from thousands of years in the past to thousands of years in the future.

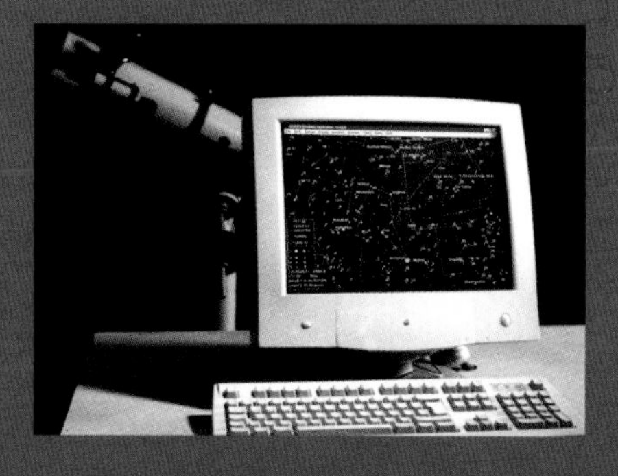

A home computer can be linked by cable to a telescope with a suitable mounting. Increasingly, telescopes come with their own hand-held computer-control units.

Refracting telescopes and binoculars

The simplest telescope designs are based around lenses that refract, or bend, light to a focus. A lens is simply a curved piece of glass that changes the direction of light rays passing through it. Simple convex lenses bulge outward in the middle and are thinner around the edge. As a result, the refraction effect becomes greater toward the edge of the lens, and all the light rays passing through it can be brought to a single focus.

Very early refracting telescopes used just two convex lenses—an objective to bend light to a focus and an eyepiece to magnify it and divert it into the observer's eye. A major problem with this design is that a convex lens bends different colors of light by different amounts. This causes multicolored "fringes" to appear around the image it produces. In order to eliminate these, most designs now use additional concave lenses to ensure that all the different colors come to a focus at the same point.

The simplest refractor telescopes are just tubes with a lens at each end. The magnifying power of the eyepiece depends on its position in regard to the path of light through the telescope. For this reason, small refracting telescopes are often made with two or more nested tubes, allowing the eyepiece to slide back and forth. In most telescopes, the eyepiece is fixed securely in position and is often fitted onto a "rack and pinion" mechanism that uses a sort of gear setup to allow for minute adjustments.

Binoculars are really just two refracting telescopes mounted side by side—one for each eye. Prisms bounce the path of light internally, so the barrels of fairly powerful binoculars can be compact. Light rays gathered inside any optical instrument cross over at the focus, so the image they produce is upside down. Binoculars, and some telescopes for daytime use, have extra lenses to correct this problem. Astronomical telescopes ignore this issue because the extra lenses required absorb valuable light—and there is no "up" or "down" in space anyway.

CUTAWAY VIEW OF THE INTERIOR OF A REFLECTING TELESCOPE IN A DOBSONIAN MOUNT

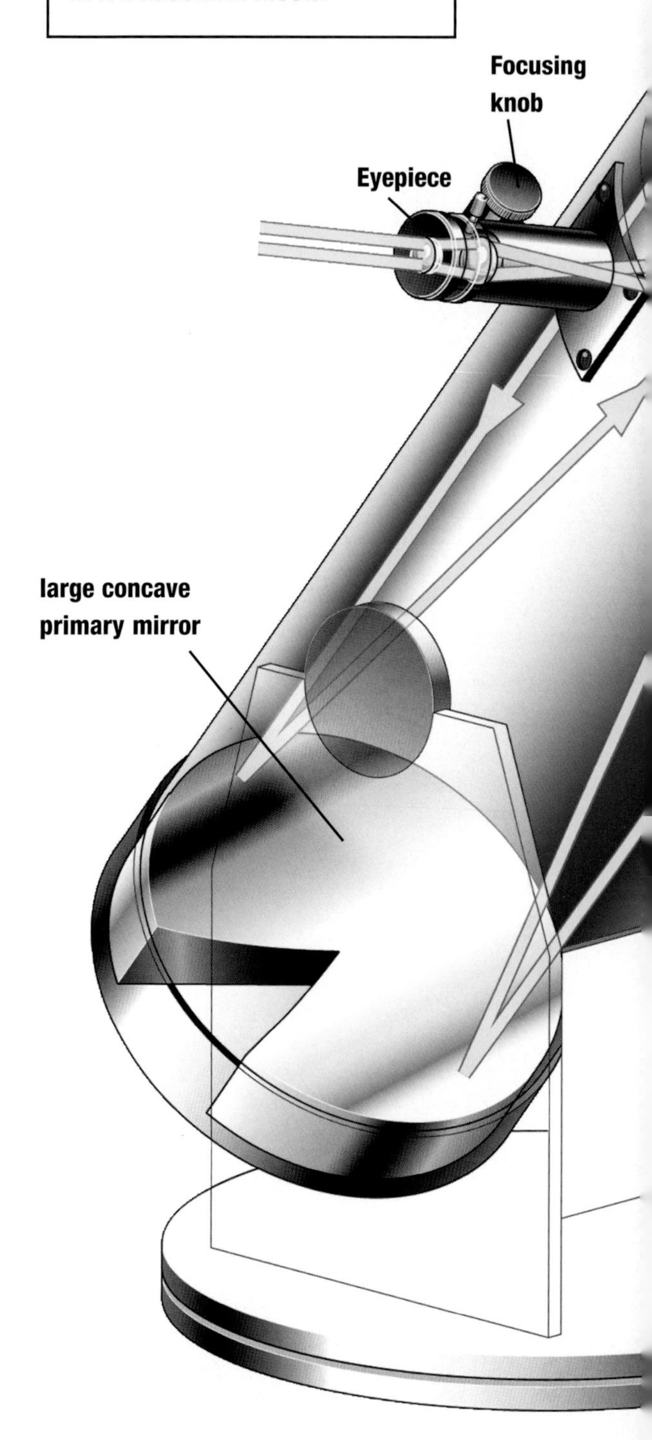

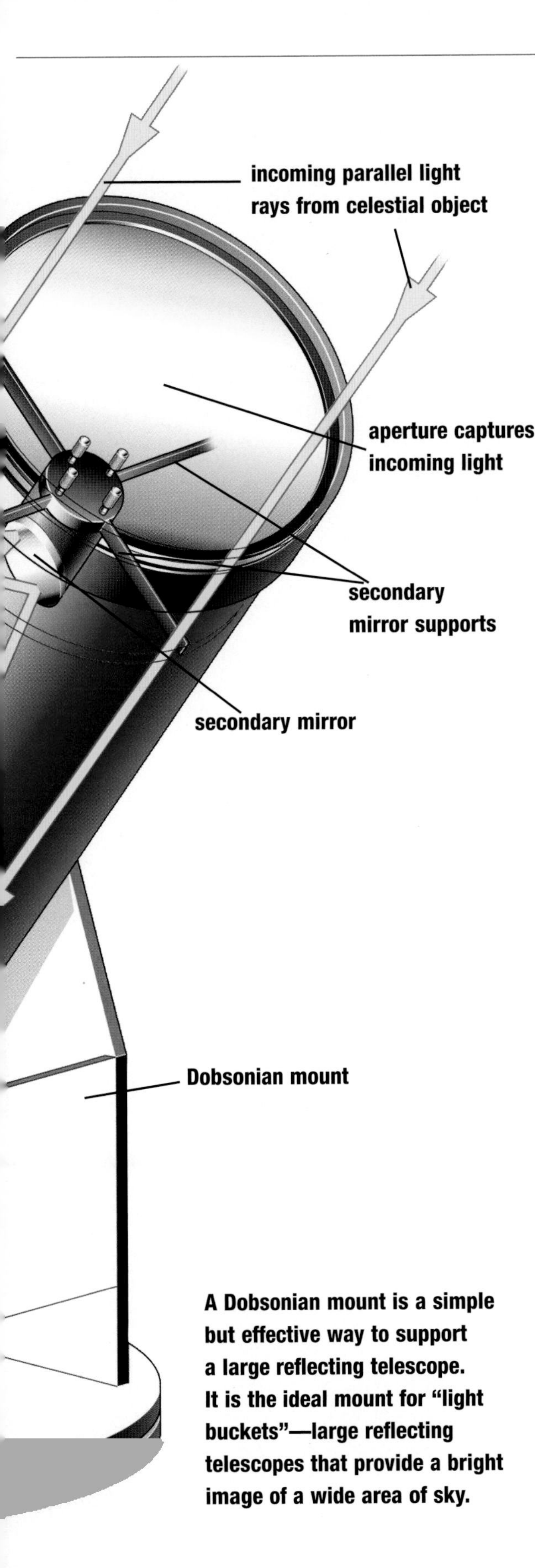

A Dobsonian mount is a simple but effective way to support a large reflecting telescope. It is the ideal mount for "light buckets"—large reflecting telescopes that provide a bright image of a wide area of sky.

Reflecting telescopes

Reflecting telescopes have some important advantages over refractors, but also some limitations. The primary light-gathering instrument in a reflecting telescope is a mirror ground into a perfect dish-shaped "parabola" (curve) and covered with a reflective coating. Parallel rays of light hitting this mirror are reflected onto converging paths and brought to a focus. Reflectors also need at least one secondary mirror. In Newtonian reflectors, the secondary mirror deflects the light out through the side of the telescope and into the eyepiece. In Schmidt-Cassegrain reflectors, the light path bounces back up the tube and through a hole in the middle of the primary mirror.

Reflectors resolve less detail than a refractor with the same-sized aperture (the opening that lets in light). The resolving power of a telescope is its ability to separate and clarify fine details. In general, a 6-inch (150-millimeter) reflector is needed to match the performance of a 3-inch (75-mm) refractor—although both are likely to cost about the same to purchase.

Telescope mounts

The mount, or support structure for a telescope, is almost as important as the quality of its optics (lenses and/or mirrors). The two most common mounts are the alt-azimuth and equatorial designs. An alt-azimuth telescope has a relatively simple mounting that allows it to pivot in both altitude and azimuth. In other words, the telescope can move up and down or sideways. An equatorial telescope is more complex, but allows the telescope to pivot in declination (above or below the celestial equator) or in R.A. (along paths perpendicular to the celestial equator). R.A. follows the movement of objects across Earth's sky, so once an object is in the telescope's field of view, simply moving the telescope in R.A. can track it. Some telescopes have an automatic "clock drive" that turns the telescope as it tracks the movement of objects around the sky.

OBSERVING THE SOLAR SYSTEM

CHAPTER 3

The objects of the solar system are on our cosmic doorstep. They include one star (the Sun), three other rocky planets (which are more or less similar to Earth), four giant gas planets, and numerous moons. Icy Pluto, the controversial, tiny outer planet, is among countless smaller objects that include rocky asteroids and comets.

Observing the Sun

The Sun is the most obvious of all objects in the sky. Without its blazing light and heat, life on Earth could not exist. It seems to go once around the sky every day, rising in the east and setting in the west, but this is just an illusion caused by Earth's daily rotation. If that rotation could be stopped, we would see the Sun slowly moving around the sky once a year. But this, too, is an illusion created by our changing point of view. We orbit the Sun and see it against a band of different background constellations (star groups) called the zodiac.

The Sun's path through the sky is called the ecliptic. Throughout the year, it moves from 23 degrees north of Earth's (and therefore, the celestial) equator to 23 degrees south of it. The ecliptic changes in relation to Earth's equator changes because Earth tilts at 23 degrees as it rotates on its axis. At certain times of year, the Northern Hemisphere tilts toward the Sun, while at other times, the Southern Hemisphere does. In the hemisphere tilted toward the Sun, the days are longer, the Sun rises higher in the sky, and it is warmer. In the opposite hemisphere, the days are shorter, the Sun is lower in the sky, and it is cooler. Every year, the Sun reaches its extreme northern and southern points on about June 21 and December 21, respectively. These days are either the longest or shortest days of the year, depending on the hemisphere and month of year.

The space shuttle *Endeavour* took this photograph of the *Hubble Space Telescope (HST)* from orbit. The *HST* has captured some remarkable images of our own solar system as well as images of many deep-space objects.

The safest way to observe the Sun is to project its image through a telescope's lens onto a card. If the card is replaced with a notepad mounted on a suitable stand, the observer can draw and record the Sun's features.

Light from the Sun is too bright to look at directly with the naked eye or through any optical instrument. We can only study the Sun using special telescopes or by projecting an image through a telescope and onto a piece of thin cardboard. Projections can reveal sunspots on the surface of the Sun and can also show events such as solar eclipses (when the Moon passes between Earth and the Sun) and transits (when Venus or Mercury pass across the Sun's face).

Observing the Moon

The Moon is another unmistakable object in Earth's skies. It orbits Earth at an average distance of about 240,000 miles (385,000 km), and is 2,160 miles (3,476 km) across. The Moon appears to have phases because we see different amounts of its sunlit surface at different points in its orbit. A complete cycle of phases lasts 29.5 days. When the Moon is a slender crescent, just before or after the New Moon (when it is completely invisible), the dark regions of the disk can often be seen glowing slightly thanks to "Earthshine"—sunlight reflecting off Earth to light the Moon.

The Moon's orbit tilts at five degrees to the ecliptic. As a result, the Moon follows a complex path across the sky, which repeats every nineteen years. We always see the same side of the Moon from Earth. Gravitational forces have slowed the Moon's rotation so much that our natural satellite rotates on its axis in exactly the same length of time it takes to orbit Earth.

English astronomer Thomas Harriot (1560—1621) was one of the first people to look at the Moon and other celestial objects through a telescope.

Binoculars and small telescopes can reveal many of the Moon's surface features. Even with the naked eye, we can tell that the Moon's surface is a mixture of bright white regions (the highlands) and darker areas, or "seas." Binoculars show that the highlands are packed with circular craters, while the seas are gray plains with far fewer craters. Astronomers believe the seas formed billions of years ago, when volcanic lava flooded many of the Moon's largest craters. The smaller craters now visible in the seas have formed since then. Today, we know that nearly all the craters on the Moon were formed by impacts from space rocks.

The best time to see detailed features on the Moon is around lunar sunrise and sunset, when the Sun is low on the Moon's horizon and objects cast long shadows. The terminator—the line that divides day and night on the Moon—marks the sunrise or sunset region. By following the terminator line as it moves slowly across the lunar surface night by night, we can see crater rims in the highlands, mountain chains around the edge of the seas, and ripples where the lava shifted as it set. Some of the most spectacular features are the "rayed" craters—recent impact sites surrounded by rays of bright material that sprayed out during their formation.

Harriot's map (above) shows the level of detail that can easily be seen on the surface of the Moon through binoculars or a small telescope. With a steady tripod mount, even a small instrument can show many of the Moon's more interesting features.

ECLIPSES

By an amazing coincidence, the Moon and Sun appear exactly the same size in Earth's skies. In reality, the Moon is roughly four hundred times smaller than the Sun, but it is also four hundred times closer to Earth than the Sun. This means that when Earth, the Sun, and the Moon line up, an eclipse occurs. A solar eclipse occurs during a new Moon, when it passes directly between Earth and the Sun. Since the Moon's orbit does not always take it to the same place in the sky, solar eclipses do not happen at every new Moon. The alignment must also be very precise, so a total eclipse is visible from only a small area on Earth's surface, and surrounding areas see a partial solar eclipse. During a total solar eclipse, the Sun's brilliant surface is blocked out, and its thin outer atmosphere, the corona, becomes visible for a few minutes, along with flamelike flares and prominences around the Sun's edge, or limb.

Lunar eclipses occur about twice a year at full Moon, when Earth passes in front of the Sun as seen from the Moon. An eclipsed Moon is rarely completely black. As the Earth's atmosphere bends sunlight around it, the Moon usually takes on a reddish glow.

Viewing the inner planets

Mercury and Venus are considered the "inferior" planets because their orbits are closer to the Sun than Earth's orbit. These planets trace a different path around the sky than the other planets. They always stay close to the Sun, and are generally only visible in the morning and evening twilights. They are also the only planets that show obvious phases, similar to those of the Moon.

Both of the inferior planets show phases, but those on Venus are much easier to see, because the planet is much larger than Mercury and comes much closer to us. As with the Moon's phases, they occur because we see different amounts of Venus's sunlit side depending on its position in orbit. Venus is lost to us in daylight, because the planet passes close to the Sun. (On rare occasions, Mercury and Venus cross the face of the Sun itself, in an event known as a transit.)

As Venus moves away from the Sun, it appears in the morning sky, steadily drawing away from the Sun. At this time, it shows a crescent phase, growing to a "half-moon" appearance. It then draws closer to the Sun again, as it moves along the "far" side of its orbit. The phase becomes "gibbous" (between half and full). When Venus passes behind the Sun, it appears again in the evening skies, diminishing in phase from full back to crescent. Mercury takes 116 days to complete its phases and to return to the same position relative to Earth. Venus completes its cycle in 584 days. This means Venus gets much farther away from the Sun and appears as a brilliant "star" against dark skies. Unfortunately, Mercury is too small for us to discern features on its surface, and Venus is cloaked in a dense, yellowish-white atmosphere that hides its surface completely.

Viewing the outer planets

The "superior" planets are those with orbits larger than Earth's. They do not show obvious phases from Earth because we can only ever see their sun-facing sides, but they have other features that are well worth observing. The most

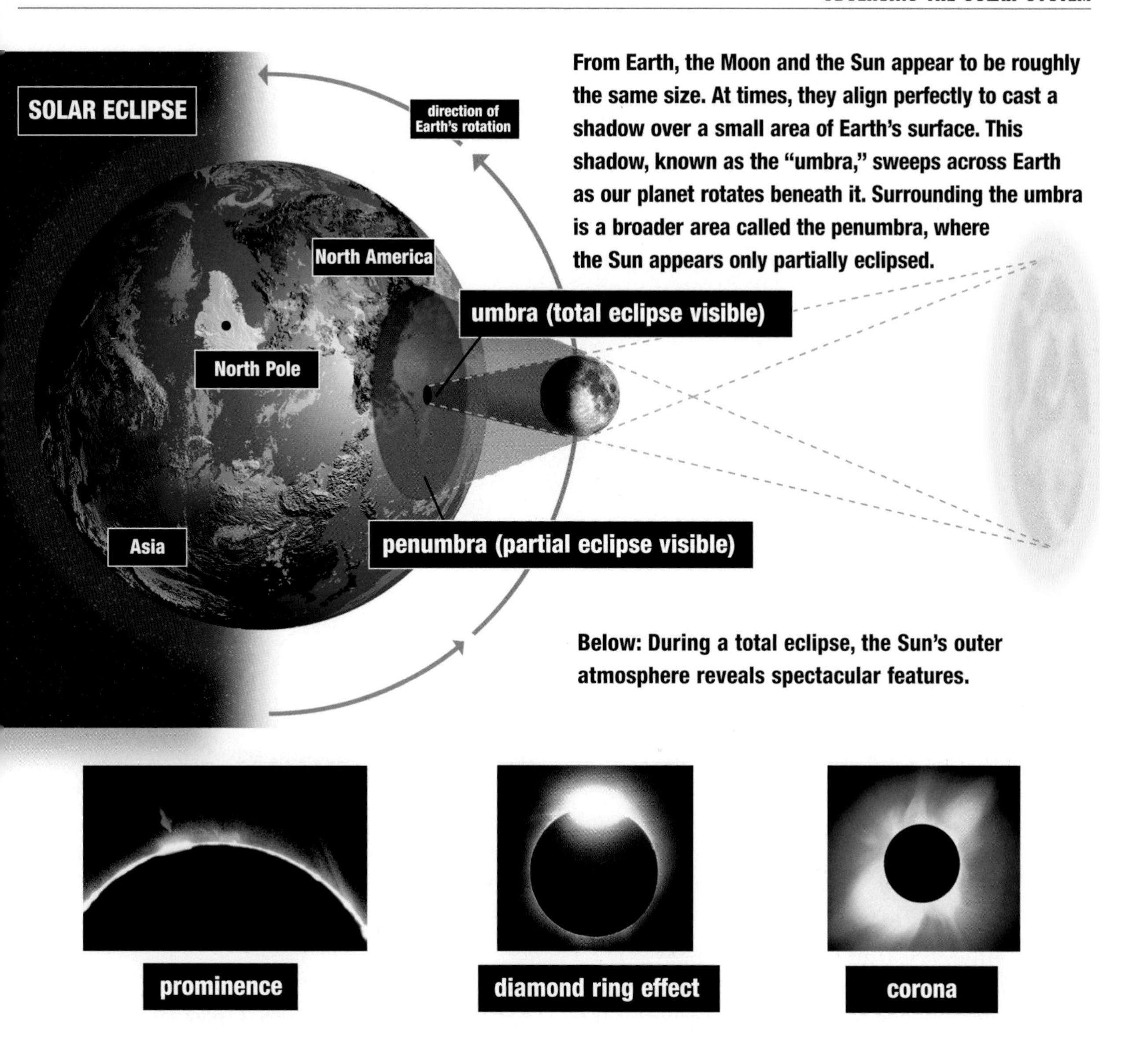

From Earth, the Moon and the Sun appear to be roughly the same size. At times, they align perfectly to cast a shadow over a small area of Earth's surface. This shadow, known as the "umbra," sweeps across Earth as our planet rotates beneath it. Surrounding the umbra is a broader area called the penumbra, where the Sun appears only partially eclipsed.

Below: During a total eclipse, the Sun's outer atmosphere reveals spectacular features.

important points on a superior planet's orbit are called opposition and conjunction. At conjunction, a planet is closer to the Sun than to Earth, so it is basically in the same area of the sky as the Sun. This means it is lost in twilight for several weeks as it disappears from the eastern morning sky and reappears in the west in the evenings. At opposition, the planet is closer to Earth than the Sun, and it is visible all night. In general, superior planets follow a path around the sky from west to east. This movement is complicated by loops of backward or "retrograde" motion, caused as Earth, moving faster in its smaller orbit, seemingly "overtakes" them. The effect is just the same as an automobile that appears to move backward when viewed from a faster, passing car.

Mars is best viewed at opposition (every two to three years), when it appears largest and brightest in our skies. At this time, the planet's white polar caps and some of the darker patches on its surface are visible through a small telescope.

Jupiter is so large that it can be viewed all year round. Binoculars reveal its four brightest satellites as they orbit the giant planet. These Galilean (discovered by Galileo) moons—Io, Europa, Ganymede, and Callisto—is each a complex world in its own right. Small telescopes

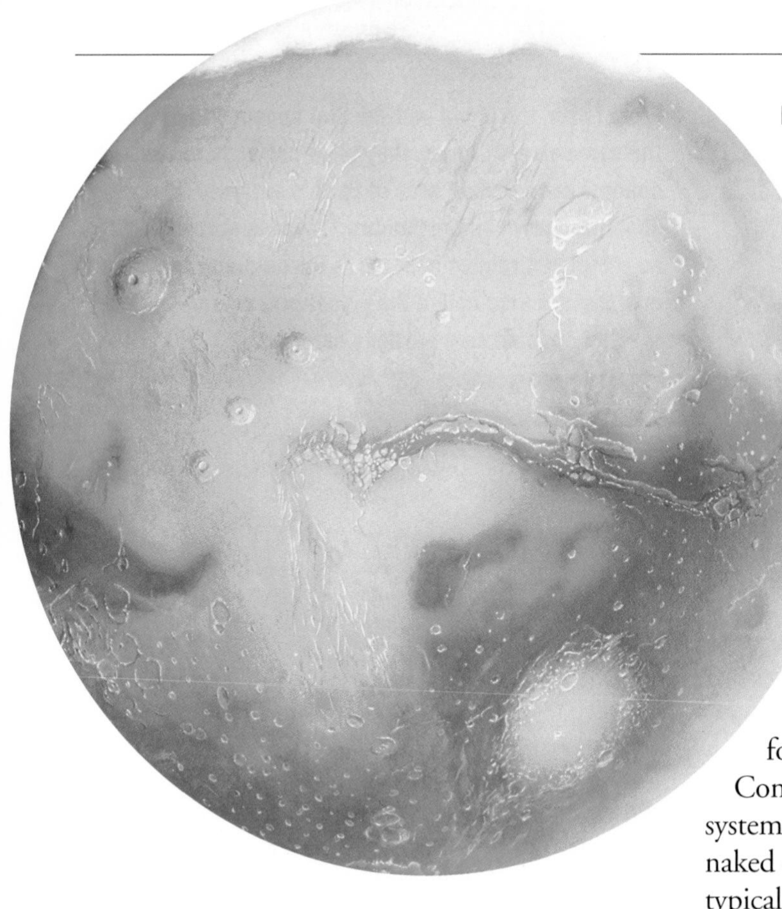

Mars's polar icecaps change their size between seasons. They are often visible as bright areas through a telescope.

reveal details of Jupiter itself, including the flattened poles caused by its rapid spin, the alternating light and dark bands of its weather systems, the shadows of satellites, and perhaps the dark oval of the Great Red Spot—a storm system large enough to swallow many Earths.

Saturn is so far from Earth that its apparent size does not change much between opposition and conjunction. Saturn's most interesting and obvious features are its famous and fabulous rings. Binoculars hint that the planet's shape is not a perfect disk. A small telescope is needed to spot the gap between the planet and the rings. The telescope may also reveal a thin dark line within the rings themselves. This thin gap is called the Cassini Division. Saturn's giant moon, Titan, is also visible with binoculars.

Other worlds

Beyond the planets that can be seen with the naked eye lie many fainter objects. The largest are the outer planets. Uranus is easily seen with binoculars if you know where to look (astronomy magazines often publish sky charts). Neptune is a good target for small telescopes. Both planets are too far away to show any surface features.

Countless asteroids are scattered throughout the solar system but are concentrated mostly in the asteroid belt between Mars and Jupiter. The largest of these tiny worlds—Ceres, Vesta, Pallas, and Juno—are visible with binoculars. Consult a sky chart for where to find them.

Comets are the only other objects in the solar system that can sometimes be seen with the naked eye. These are chunks of rock and ice, typically a few miles (km) across, that become visible as they near the Sun. A comet's typical cloudlike head (called a coma), often with a long tail stretching behind it, is caused by the heat of the Sun evaporating the ice on the surface of the comet and blowing the gas away.

Bright comets are rare and unpredictable, but their appearance can be spectacular. They are so large and diffuse that they are easier to see with the naked eye or binoculars than with a telescope.

AT THE EDGE OF THE SOLAR SYSTEM

Kuiper Belt Objects (KBOs) are out of range for all but the most powerful telescopes. Also known as ice dwarfs, KBOs are the outer solar system's equivalent of asteroids. They are found in a doughnut-shaped ring beyond the orbit of Neptune. This ring is known as the Kuiper Belt. Pluto is the brightest of them, but even Pluto is more than ten thousand times fainter than the faintest naked-eye star. The only way to identify KBOs is by photographing the exact same area of sky several nights in a row and looking for anything that appears to have moved against the background stars. Such movement indicates an object is much closer to us than the stars and is following an orbit through the outer solar system. This is how Pluto was discovered in 1930. The same technique is still used today.

The Oort Cloud, a vast spherical shell of dormant comets about one light-year from the Sun, lies even farther away and is fainter than the Kuiper Belt. These tiny, dark objects are beyond the reach of even our largest telescopes. We only know they exist because many of the comets that enter the inner solar system seem to begin their journeys in this region of space.

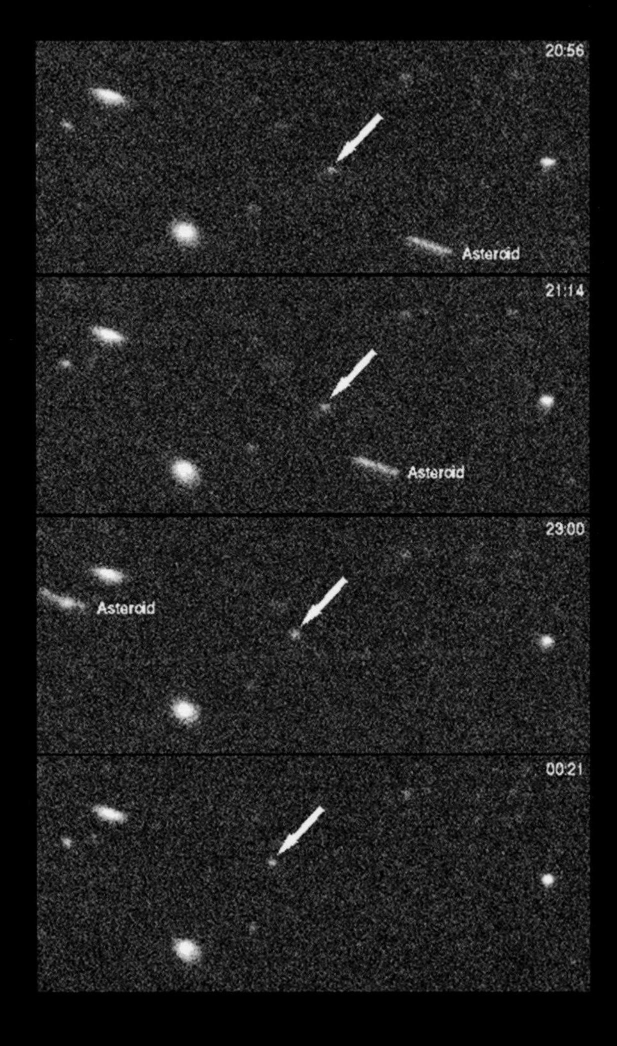

This sequence of pictures, taken by David Jewitt and Jane Luu, revealed 1992 QB1, the first KBO ever discovered. During the time interval covered by these pictures, the faint object (arrows) moved steadily across the sky, while the background stars remained virtually stationary. The bright streak in the upper two photographs was caused by a faster-moving asteroid closer to the Sun.

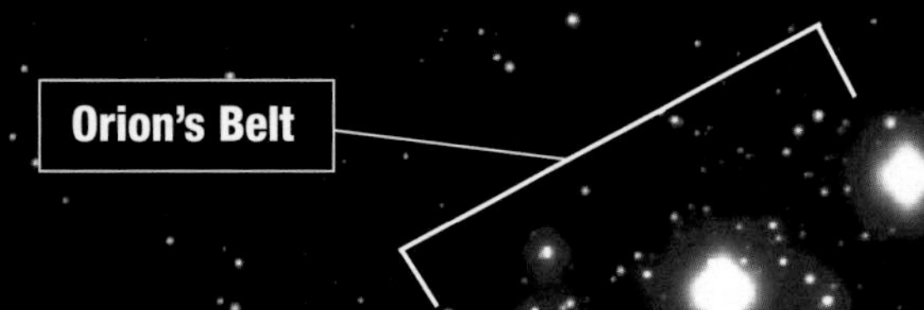
Betelgeuse
Orion's Belt

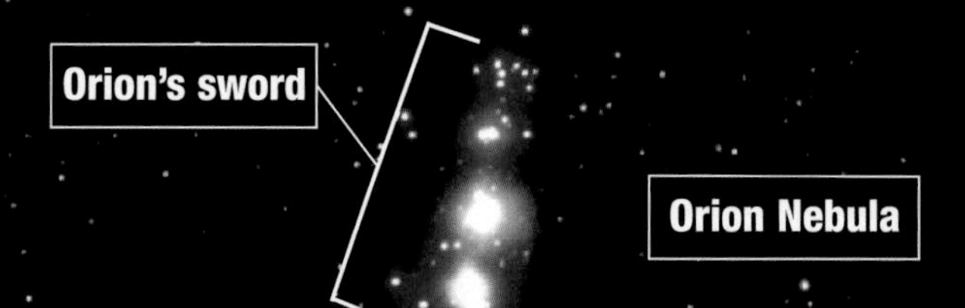
Orion's sword
Orion Nebula
Rigel

CHAPTER 4

OBSERVING THE STARS

Every star in the sky is a sun much like our own. So unimaginably distant that all stars appear only as a point of light, they have nonetheless fascinated people throughout history. Even though stars are moving rapidly through space, they appear "fixed" from our point of view because they are so very far from Earth. Telescopes allow us to observe their behavior in more detail.

Constellations and the Names of Stars

For early astronomers, the apparent immobility of stars made them natural reference points for objects that move through the sky, such as the Sun, the Moon, and the planets. Constellations, the apparent patterns made by stars (as seen from Earth), probably originated from mythmaking and storytelling, but still form the basis for many sky catalogs.

We now recognize a total of eighty-eight constellations. Ptolemy drew up an original list of forty-eight constellations from the time of the classical world (*see pages 5–6*). During the 1700s, the list of constellations grew, especially for the southern skies. At first, the constellations were simply the patterns of stars joined up to make certain "pictures," but many disagreements occurred over which stars to include and which to leave out. The invention of the telescope revealed many more stars in each region of the sky.

Finally, in 1922, the International Astronomical Union (IAU), the governing body of world astronomy, redefined the constellations of areas of sky with precise boundaries. This means that astronomers throughout the globe agree that every star or other celestial object now belong to a specific constellation, even if they are far away from one of the traditional patterns.

The bright stars of the constellation Orion are a memorable sight during northern winter nights. This long-exposure photograph captures the intense light of stars such as Betelgeuse and Rigel, as well as the fainter details of the Orion Nebula.

Bright stars have had individual names since the earliest times, but the first attempt to classify them properly was made by German astronomer Johann Bayer (1572–1625) in 1603. He named the brightest star in each constellation with the first letter of the Greek alphabet ("alpha"), the second-brightest ("beta"), and so on, through all twenty-four Greek letters. In 1725, British Astronomer Royal John Flamsteed (1646–1719) extended the catalog by numbering the unlettered stars from west to east across each constellation. Although the system seems confusing and has mistakes in it, this patchwork of different names is still widely used. There are also several catalogs of brighter stars. The most popular is the Henry Draper (HD) catalog, which gives each star a unique HD number.

Stellar highlights

It's impossible to list all the interesting stars in the sky. The sections that follow offer some information about the brightest stars and about some of the most interesting multiple and variable stars.

The brightest stars

The brightest stars in Earth's skies are prominent for one of two reasons: either they are far away and unusually bright, or they are relatively average, nearby stars. The brightest stars in the sky include examples of many different types of stars.

Sirius (in the constellation Canis Major) is a white star, about twenty times brighter than the Sun, but also very nearby—just 8 light-years from Earth. Sirius has a faint companion star called Sirius B. This is a "white dwarf," and is all that remains of a larger companion Sirius once had. Sirius B, however, is very faint and tends to get lost in the light of the brighter star.

Canopus (in the constellation Carina) is a white supergiant star, 100 light-years away. It is much farther away than Sirius, but shines as brightly as 10,000 Suns. Because of Canopus's great mass and density, it burns through its supply of hydrogen at a faster rate than does our Sun.

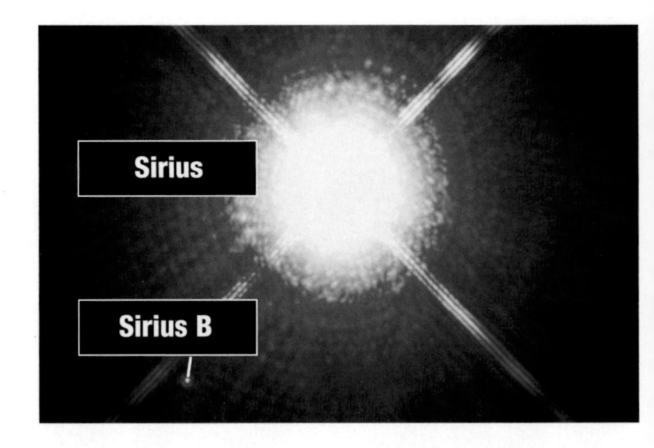

Above: The brilliant light of Sirius, the dog star, drowns out its much fainter companion, Sirius B.

Below: Red giants can grow to an immense size. If we could place Betelgeuse in the center of our solar system, it would extend past the orbit of Mars.

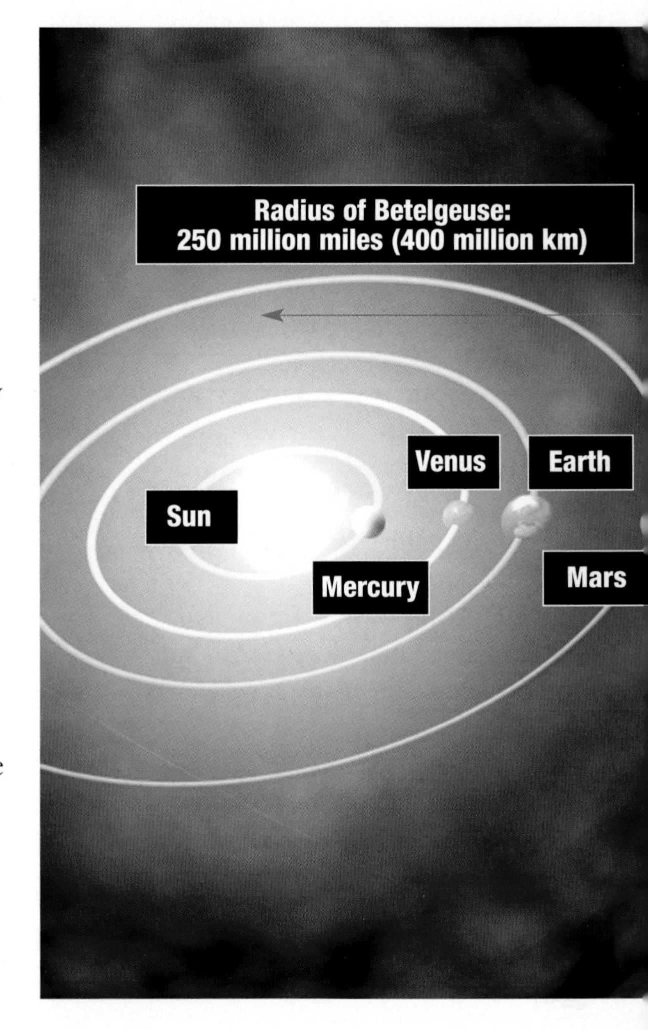

The Alpha Centauri system, 4.3 light-years away, contains our nearest stellar neighbors. To the naked eye, it appears as a single star, but binoculars or a small telescope reveal that it is two stars, consisting of a bright-yellow, sunlike star (roughly twice the brightness of the Sun) and a slightly fainter orange one. The closest star to Earth is a very dim "red dwarf" star called Proxima Centauri.

Arcturus (in the constellation Boötes), an orange giant star, is a sunlike star nearing the end of its life. It shines with the brightness of seventy of our Suns and is 37 light-years away.

Vega (in the constellation Lyra) is a white main-sequence star. Brighter than Sirius with the luminosity of forty-eight Suns, it lies 25 light-years away. A ring of dust left over from its birth, where planets may be forming, surrounds it.

Rigel (in the constellation Orion), with the brightness of 44,000 Suns, is among the most luminous stars. A white supergiant approaching the end of its life, Rigel lies 860 light-years away. Deneb (in the constellation Cygnus) is even more extreme, shining as brightly as 250,000 Suns—but from a distance of 3,000 light-years.

Betelgeuse (also in the constellation Orion) is a red supergiant. It appears slightly fainter than Arcturus, but is actually more than one hundred times brighter, and 400 light-years away. This dying star is much more massive than the Sun or Arcturus.

Beta Centauri is a blue star whose compact, heavy mass makes it burn through its fuel supply faster, causing it to shine more brightly. It is 500 light-years away, and as bright as 12,000 Suns.

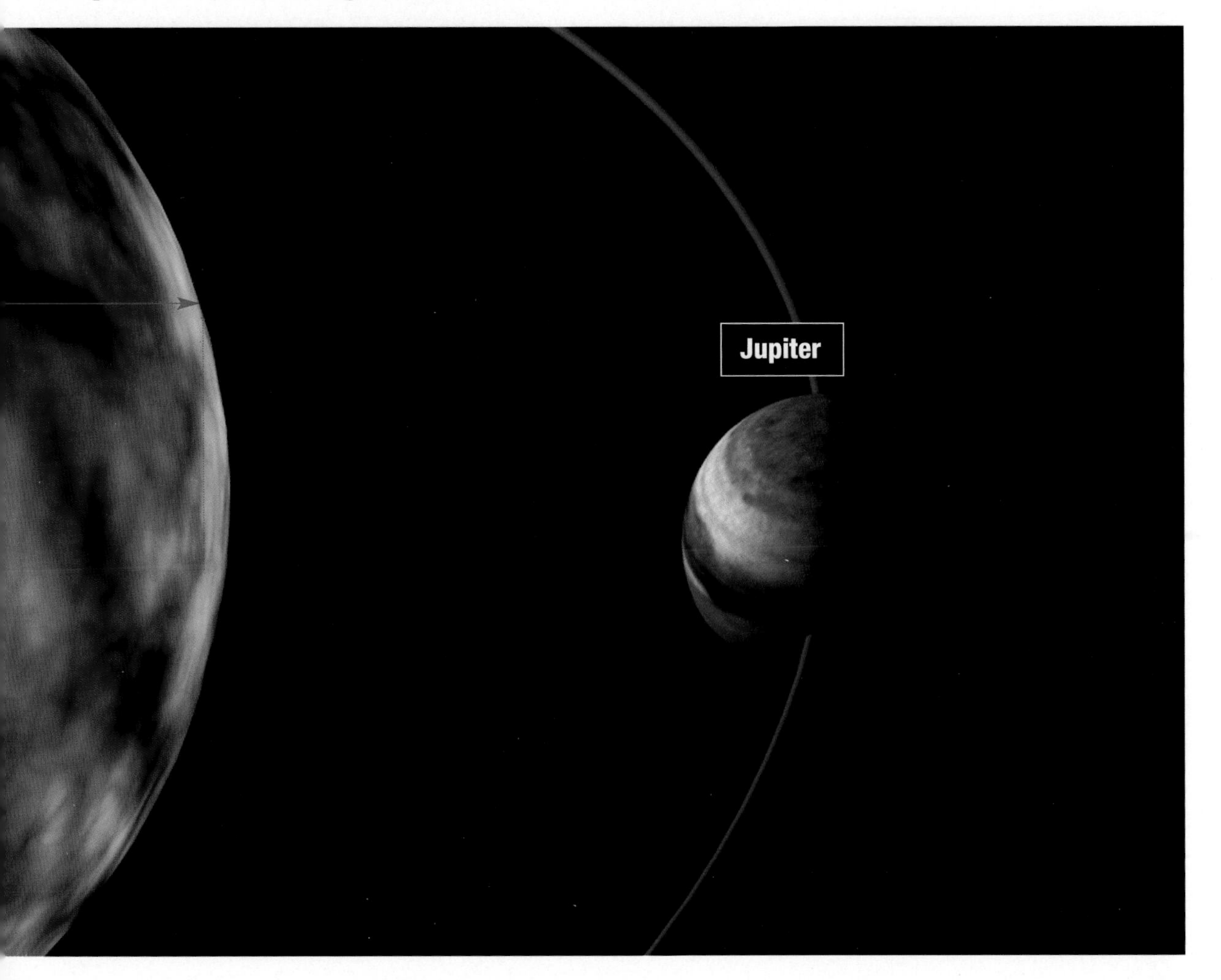

EXTREME STARS

Some stars are so dim or so small that they can only be seen with professional equipment. Astronomers have recently been discovering that the galaxy is full of extremely faint red dwarfs, which are generally too dim to see if they are not nearby, and brown dwarfs, which are "failed stars" that barely emit any light at all but produce infrared (heat) radiation. There are also several types of star that are extremely hot and bright, but so tiny that their size makes them difficult to spot. White dwarfs (such as Sirius B) are one example of these super-dense remains of stars. They are white-hot stars about the size of Earth. Even more extreme are neutron stars, which are far hotter and brighter than white dwarfs, but just a few miles across. Intense magnetic fields surround neutron stars. This channels their radiation into two narrow beams that sweep around like a stellar lighthouse as the star rotates. Radio telescopes on Earth detect this invisible radiation as pulses, giving neutron stars their other name: Pulsars.

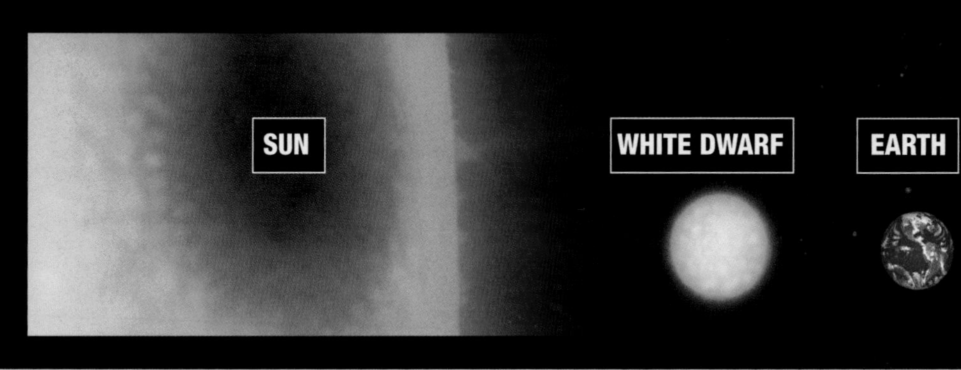

Bright Doubles

Double stars are common in the sky. Many of these may, in fact, be many light-years apart, but just happen to lie in the same plane of space as seen from Earth. A large number of stars, however, are truly double or multiple. Doubles or multiples occur when two or more stars that formed from the same cloud of gas are caught up in orbit around each other. Some of the most prominent double stars are listed below:

Albireo (in the constellation Cygnus) is one of the most colorful doubles in the sky. Binoculars can help a viewer separate its two stars. The brighter is a yellow giant nearing the end of its life, while the fainter is an unusual blue-green star.

Mizar, the middle star in the handle of the Big Dipper (an asterism in the constellation Ursa Major) has a nearby companion called Alcor. The two stars just happen to lie in the same plane of space and are not a true binary. A small telescope reveals that Mizar is a binary in its own right, and each of the other three stars are themselves doubles.

Epsilon Lyrae is a famous "double double" star: two binary pairs of stars in orbit around each other. While binoculars can help you separate the pairs from each other, use a telescope to "split" the individual pairs.

LEARNING FROM DOUBLE STARS

Binary stars offer astronomers a unique chance to measure the properties of stars, such as weight, mass, and age. The stars of a binary system are locked in orbit around a pivot point, known as their common center of mass (barycenter), which is always closer to the heavier star. By measuring the orbits of the stars—either visually or from the back-and-forth movement of their spectral lines (*see* Spectroscopy *box, page 12*), astronomers can determine the masses of the two stars. Since both stars began their lives at the same time, astronomers can figure out how a star's mass affects its aging.

Star Clusters

Many of the stars in the sky are found in large clusters. These fall into two general types: loose open clusters and tightly packed globular clusters.

Open clusters can contain anything from a few dozen to a few hundred stars, often blue and white in color. The stars within an open cluster are very young and are sometimes still surrounded by the glowing gas and dust from which they formed. Over time, open clusters disintegrate as the stars within them move apart.

Globular clusters contain hundreds of thousands, or even millions, of stars. As the name suggests, the stars are packed together in a ball shape. These clusters seem to follow their own orbit around our galaxy. They are often found in the relatively empty "halo" above and below the Milky Way. The stars within them are red and yellow in color. They are very old and have kept their structure for many billions of years. Some of the most interesting clusters in the sky are listed below:

The Pleiades (in Taurus) form a dense cluster of blue-white stars known as "the seven sisters." This cluster contains about one hundred members, of which six or seven are visible to the naked eye.

The Hyades (in Taurus) form a V-shaped cluster, which is older and more scattered than the Pleiades. It is easy to spot because the bright red giant, Aldebaran, happens to lie in the same direction.

The Jewel Box (in Crux) is a spectacular group of several dozen stars gathered around a red supergiant. At a mere seven million years old, it is one of the youngest clusters known.

M13 (in Hercules) is a globular cluster containing about three hundred thousand stars packed into a ball about 100 light-years across.

Omega Centauri is the largest-known globular cluster. It is 650 light-years across and contains several million stars.

The central stars of the Pleiades are still surrounded by some of the gas and dust from which they were born.

NEBULAE

The space between the stars is filled with huge clouds of gas and dust that astronomers call nebulae. Young stars are born in nebulae. When old, dying stars cast off their outer layers, they replenish the nebulae. There are several types of nebulae, and the type we see partly depends on the angle at which we view it.

Emission nebulae are places where stars are born. Here, the fierce radiation from young stars heats up the gas around them until it glows. Although photographs often show them as pink in color, they look green through a small telescope. This occurs because the human eye has trouble detecting low levels of red light. The Great Nebula in the middle of Orion's sword, and the Lagoon Nebula in Sagittarius are fine examples of emission nebulae.

Dark nebulae are clouds of dust and gas that do not glow but only show up when silhouetted against a brighter background. The Horsehead Nebula in Orion, close to the Great Nebula, is the most famous example. Two other naked-eye dark nebulae are easy to spot. One is the "Great Rift," which blocks out part of the Milky Way in Cygnus, and the other is "Coal Sack" in Crux, the Southern Cross.

Reflection nebulae are created when dust clouds happen to reflect the light of nearby stars in our direction. A good example is the faint nebula around the Pleiades star cluster in Taurus. From other directions, it would be invisible, and might even appear as a dark nebula.

Planetary nebulae are regions of glowing gas thrown off by a red giant star in the last stages of its life. They are different from other nebulae because they are compact and often ring-shaped. The most famous is the Ring Nebula in Lyra.

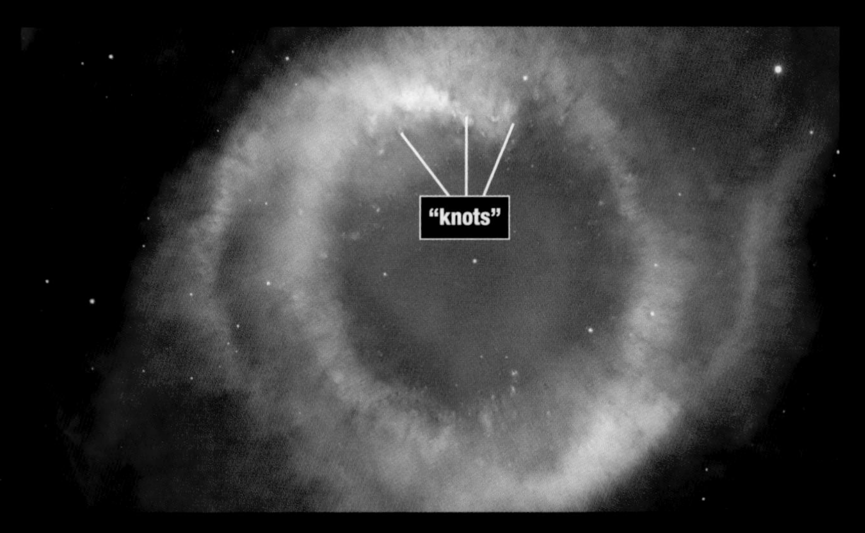

The Helix Nebula, 450 light-years away, is a beautiful planetary nebula. Different colors highlight the different elements in the ejected gas. The "knots" in the gas are caused where rapidly expanding hot gas has overtaken cooler, slower-moving material.

Interesting variables

Quite a number of stars change their appearance more or less regularly, with occasional brief dips in brightness, sudden bursts of light, or a slow and steady variation between a minimum and maximum brightness. Variable stars are easiest to observe by comparing them with other nearby stars that have a more constant brightness. Some of the most prominent are listed below:

Algol (in Perseus) is an eclipsing binary with two stars in close orbit around each other. Every 2.9 days, the fainter star passes in front of the brighter one, and Algol drops in brightness for a few hours.

Mira (in Cetus) is a pulsating variable with a long period (cycle of brightness variations) lasting about eleven months. It is a red giant star and is easily spotted at maximum brightness, but is invisible, even through binoculars, at its minimum.

Delta Cephei (in Cepheus) is a yellow supergiant. It is a pulsating "Cepheid" variable that changes its size and brightness in a five-day cycle. The brighter periods of such a variable are much shorter than its dimmer ones.

Eta Carinae (in Carina)—a supergiant star surrounded by gas that it has thrown off into space—is an unpredictable variable. Normally, it shines on the limits of visibility to the naked eye, but in 1843, it unexpectedly became the second-brightest star in the sky.

Eta Carinae, embedded in clouds of material that it has already ejected, is an unstable star nearing the end of its life. Eventually, it will destroy itself in a supernova.

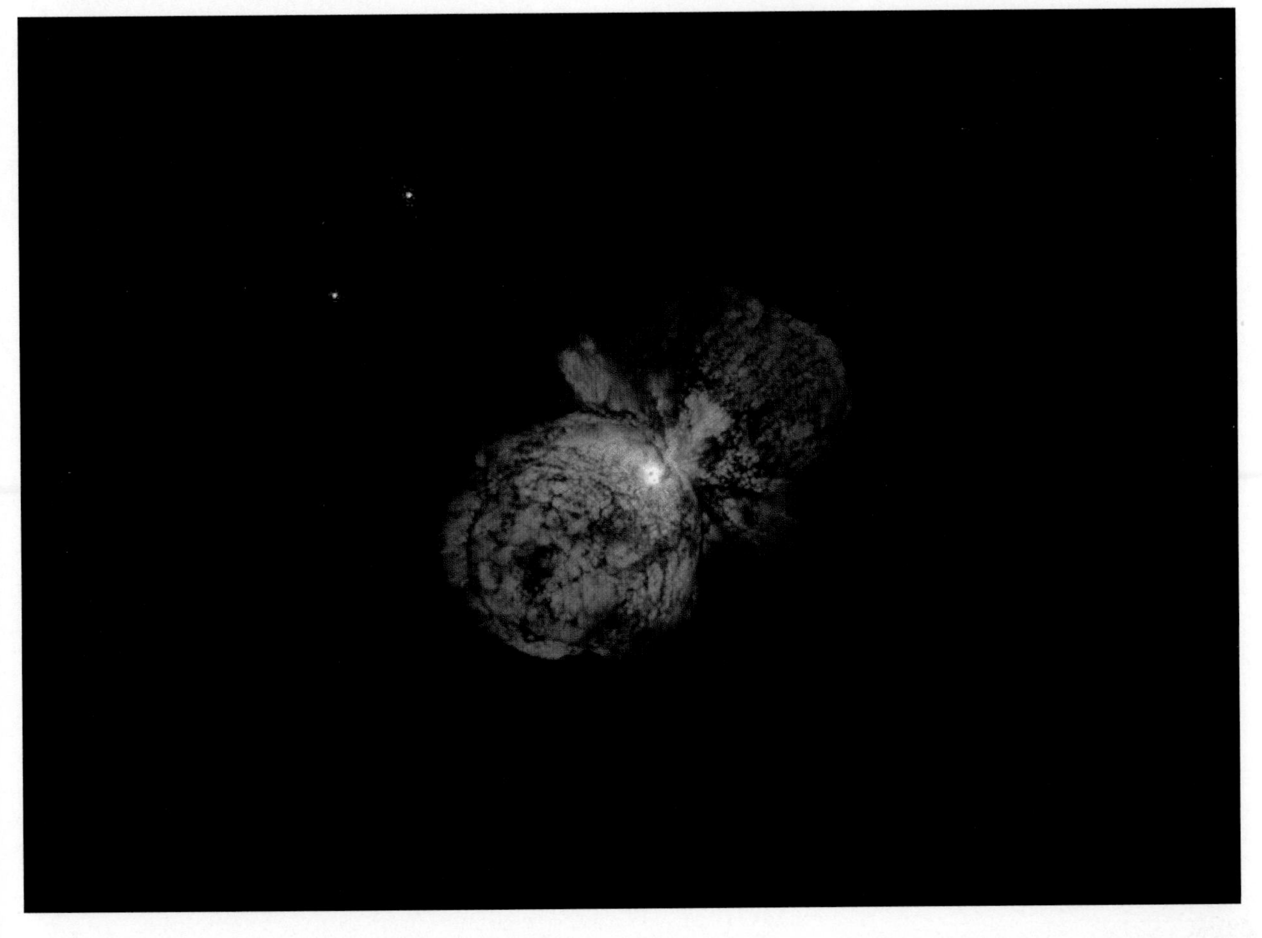

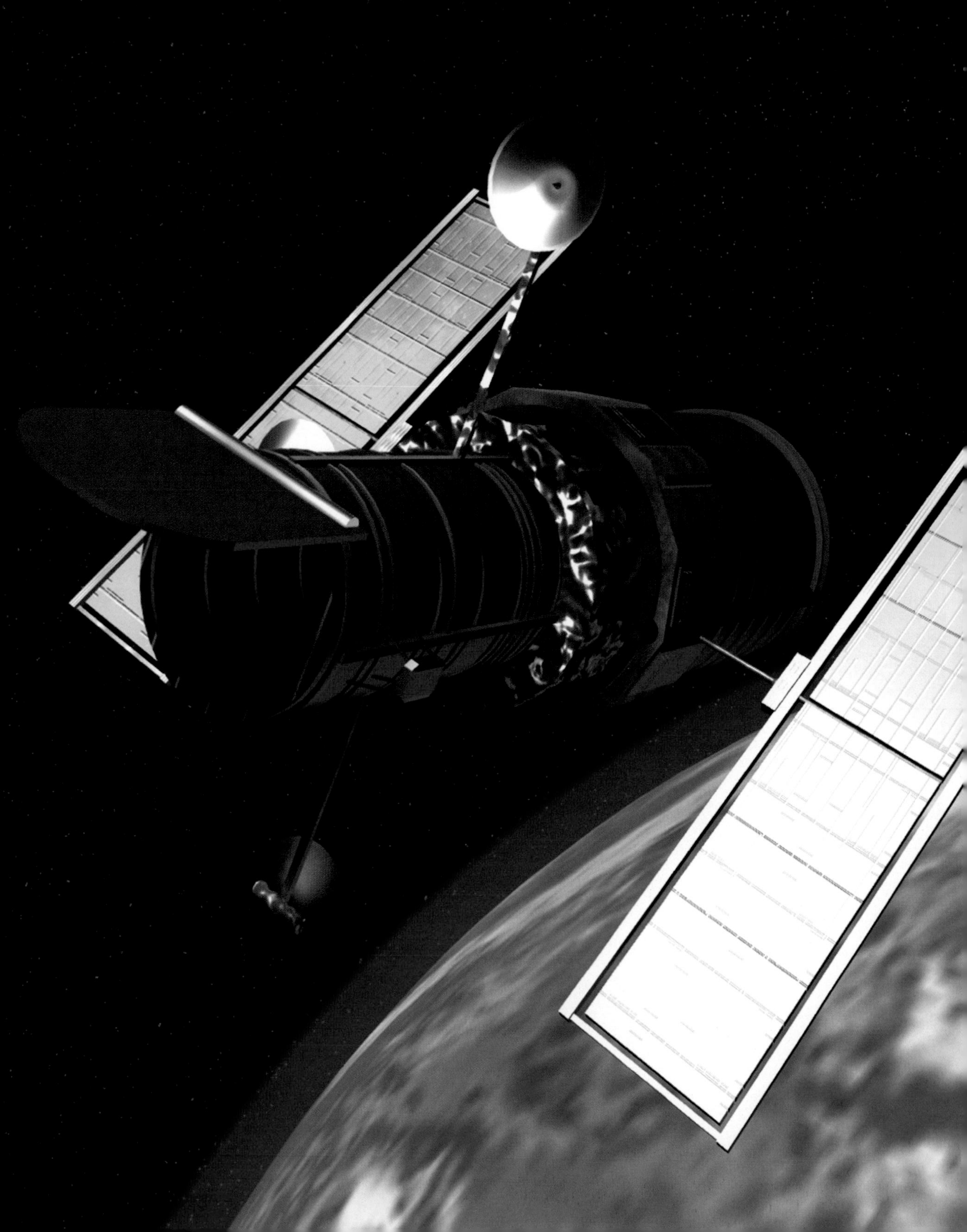

CHAPTER 5

SUPER ASTRONOMY

Professional astronomers study the limits of the universe, from mighty stellar explosions to faint planets orbiting other stars and distant galaxies at the edge of the cosmos. The telescopes they use often apply the same principles as the reflecting telescopes described in Chapter 2, but these are much bigger, computerized instruments that use the latest advanced technology to get the best images from space. The same principles can also detect other types of radiation from cool to extremely hot objects. Telescopes that operate at these wavelengths look very different, and many can only function from above Earth's atmosphere.

Giant telescopes

Since its invention, astronomers have been developing telescopes with ever-increasing sizes of lenses and mirrors. The larger a telescope is, the greater its light-collecting area and the higher its power to clarify (resolve) small details. The lens telescope reached its peak with the 40-inch (102-centimeter) refractor at the Yerkes Observatory, in Williams Bay, Wisconsin, which was completed in 1897. Reflecting telescopes, meanwhile, continued to grow in size until the middle of the twentieth century. The giant 200-inch (5-meter) reflector on Mount Palomar in California was completed in 1948. The Soviet Union built an even bigger 240-inch (6-m) reflector telescope in the 1970s, but this never performed as well as hoped. Once a telescope's lens got larger than 200 inches (5 m), it seemed that the problems of grinding and supporting a mirror could not be solved.

Today, a new generation of telescopes has overcome the problem in a variety of ingenious ways. The twin Keck Telescopes sit on top of the extinct Mauna Kea volcano on the Big Island of Hawaii.

The 1990 launch of the *Hubble Space Telescope* revolutionized astronomy. From its vantage point in orbit (unobstructed by Earth's atmosphere), *Hubble* has a clear view of the universe.

The twin domes of the 400-inch (10-m) Keck Telescopes are part of a "telescope park" on top of Mauna Kea, Hawaii—an island in a sea of clouds. Here, they are above much of Earth's atmosphere.

This location is so high that it reaches above most of the atmosphere's water vapor and cloud cover, ensuring the maximum number of clear nights and the best possible conditions for visibility. At lower altitudes, movements of air in the atmosphere blur our view of the sky, which is what causes the stars to "twinkle" in the night sky. Like the Keck Telescopes, most modern large telescopes are built on mountaintops at other sites that include La Palma in the Canary Islands, situated in the Atlantic Ocean off the northwestern coast of Africa, and the Paranal Observatory, on top of Cerro Paranal in northern Chile.

The first of the Keck Telescopes was completed in 1993. They both have 400-inch (10-m) mirrors, each made of 36 hexagonal segments. Astronomers overcame the problem of dealing with mirrors larger than 200 inches (5 m) by constructing the mirror out of hexagons. These fit together like the cells of a honeycomb, and any minute distortions that occur as the telescope aims in different directions are corrected by a system of computer-controlled "actuators." These actuators work independently and are located on pads that support each of the mirror cells from beneath.

The Keck telescopes were deliberately built as a pair to pioneer a new technique called optical interferometry. This is an optical equivalent of radio interferometry, which has been used for many years to boost the resolution of radio telescopes. The principle is simple: Two or more telescopes look at the same object, and their signals are combined. Working together, the Kecks have the same resolution (although not the light-gathering power) of a single telescope with a 280-foot (85-m) diameter.

Interferometry is also used in the Very Large Telescope (VLT) in Chile. Here, four 320-inch (8-m) diameter telescopes, along with three 72-inch (1.8-m) ones, create a virtual telescope with the resolving power of a single 390-foot (120-m) mirror. The makers of the large VLT telescopes used revolutionary new techniques to create extremely thin one-piece mirrors, which must be supported by actuators to control their shape. The VLT also uses a system of "adaptive optics"

(AO) to correct atmospheric distortions. With AO, a laser beam projects an artificial "star" into the sky near the telescope's target for comparison while a computer system monitors the atmospheric distortion, and constantly adjusts the mirror's shape to produce a perfect image of the actual star being studied.

A telescope in space

The world's most famous telescope is undoubtedly the *Hubble Space Telescope* (*HST*), launched in 1990, which is still returning stunning images from orbit. Also affectionately known as *Hubble*, it is relatively small by today's standards—the *HST*'s primary mirror is just 104 inches (2.4 m) across, but its position above Earth's atmosphere provides outstandingly clear views. Even the largest and highest Earth-based telescopes eventually run into limits on their resolution due to the movement of the Earth's atmosphere, and no system available today can remove all the distortions this causes.

A set of ground-controlled gyroscopes keep the *HST* steady in space. Its basic design is similar to a ground-based reflector, with light reflected through a hole in the center of the primary mirror and into a variety of detectors. The *HST* was designed to undergo maintenance and be upgraded in orbit. Three space shuttle missions have retrieved and serviced the *HST* in 1993, 1997, and 2002. The *HST*'s current instruments include two visible light cameras, a spectrograph for capturing the spectra of distant objects, and an infrared detector for measuring heat radiation.

Unfortunately, problems with the space shuttle may prevent another servicing mission, and if the *HST*'s stabilizers fail, it will stop working. Plans for its infrared successor, the *James Webb Space Telescope*, with a 20-foot (6.5-m) mirror, are under development. The projected launch date is after June 2013.

This famous image from *Hubble* captures the Hourglass Nebula, a planetary nebula 8,000 light-years away.

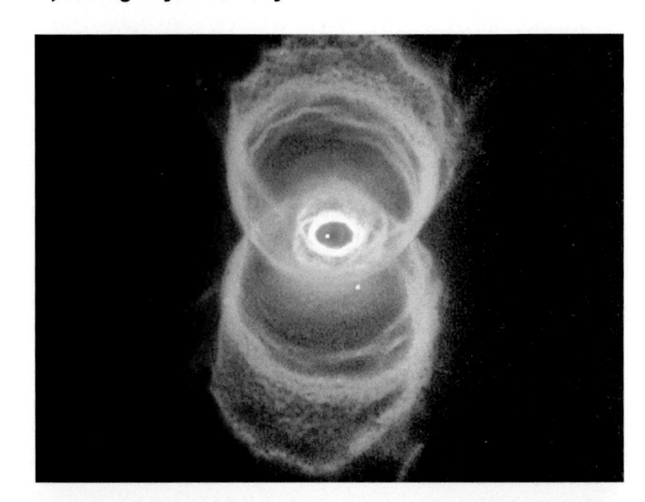

LYMAN SPITZER

American astrophysicist Lyman Spitzer (1914–1997) was the driving force behind the development and launch of the *Hubble Space Telescope.* He first pointed out the advantages of a space-based telescope in 1946, more than a decade before the beginning of the space age. He was involved in the design of many early astronomical satellites, but continued to lobby NASA and the U.S. Congress for a large visible-light telescope. The project was finally approved in 1977. Spitzer also made the first detailed studies of the gas and dust from which stars form.

Radio telescopes

Visible light, which is just one type of electromagnetic radiation, is actually made up of a combination of electrical and magnetic disturbances that reinforce each other as they travel through space. Different types of radiation have distinct wavelengths. For example, visible light ranges from 700 nanometers (billionths of a millimeter) for red colors to 390 nm for violet. Radiations with longer wavelengths than visible light are classed as infrared and radio waves. Those with shorter wavelengths are ultraviolet, X-rays, and gamma rays. Objects in space emit radiation of all these types, but most are blocked by Earth's atmosphere. Radio waves, with wavelengths longer than 1 mm (that's about 1/25 of an inch), are the only other type of radiation (besides visible light) that can be studied from Earth's surface.

U.S. engineer Karl Jansky (1905–1950) discovered the first radio signals from space in the 1930s. He used an array of radio antennas similar to those on a radio receiver. He could only guess the direction of a signal, but realized that it peaked when the Milky Way was directly overhead. A few years later, another U.S. engineer, Grote Reber (1911–2002), built a dish-shaped antenna that collected radio signals from a large area of sky and brought them to a focus, using the same principle as a reflecting telescope. This kind of receiver allowed him to determine the direction of the signals for the first time. Dish receivers are still used today.

The major challenge for radio astronomy is the comparatively huge wavelengths involved. Any telescope's resolving power depends on its size compared to the wavelengths of radiation it receives. This means that even huge dishes like the 1,000-foot (300-m) Arecibo radio dish in Puerto Rico have low resolution because the radio waves they receive are wavelengths millions of times longer than visible light. Sir Bernard Lovell (*see box, page 43*) pioneered the first giant radio telescopes in the United Kingdom.

Interferometry offers the solution to this problem. It is a method of combining the electronic signals from two or more telescopes studying the same object simultaneously. At first, the interferometry telescopes had to be physically linked. This was the reason behind the construction of the enormous Very Large Array (VLA) project, which uses twenty-seven 82-foot (25-m) dishes arranged on Y-shaped tracks in the desert of New Mexico. At maximum separation, these dishes have a combined resolution equivalent to a single 22-mile (36-km) dish. Today, such links are electronic, and a computer processes the data.

This so-called "Very Long Baseline Interferometry" (VLBI) setup can create virtual radio telescopes thousands of miles across.

Right: Jodrell Bank in northern England, one of the world's largest steerable telescopes. Almost fifty years after its completion, it is now known as the Lovell Telescope.

Below: An aerial photograph of the VLA in the New Mexico desert shows twenty-four of the array's twenty-seven telescopes.

LOVELL TELESCOPE

British astronomer Sir Bernard Lovell (b. 1913) was a pioneer of radio astronomy in the 1950s, and the driving force behind the construction of Jodrell Bank, a 250-ft (76-m) dish in Cheshire in northern England. It was the first radio telescope that could be steered. Lovell worked tirelessly to raise funds for the project. It was on the verge of cancellation in late 1957, when the Soviet Union launched its first satellite, *Sputnik,* and the space age began. Satellite tracking and communication with spacecraft became an important new use for radio telescopes, and Jodrell Bank got the boost in funding it needed. Lovell went on to detect the radio emissions from meteors in Earth's atmosphere and studied the Sun at radio wavelengths for the first time. He also discovered a new type of variable star, called a flare star, that emits radio waves.

Orbiting observatories

Telescopes that study the universe at other wavelengths do not have to cope with the size problems of radio astronomy, but they face different challenges. Most high-energy radiation never reaches Earth's surface because our protective atmosphere blocks them. While this is good for life on Earth, it's annoying for astronomers. Infrared (heat radiation) signals are also blocked or simply swamped by the general warmth of the atmosphere. The best way to study these wavelengths is to use a telescope in Earth orbit that is remote-controlled by astronomers on Earth.

The first orbiting observatories, launched in the early 1970s, studied the sky in near-ultraviolet light. Most stars (such as the Sun) produce some ultraviolet radiation, but their peak radiation is at visible wavelengths. Only a few massive and brilliant stars emit most of their energy in ultraviolet wavelengths.

Shorter wavelengths—extreme ultraviolet, X-rays, and gamma rays—are generally produced by superhot or extremely violent phenomena. For example, the gas found within galaxy clusters, at temperatures of many millions of degrees, shines at X-ray wavelengths. Material being pulled into a black hole—an infinitely dense region of space such as a collapsed star, from which not even light can escape—is also heated so much that it emits X-rays. Gamma rays, meanwhile, are produced by giant black holes at the heart of some galaxies, by supernovas (huge explosions that end the lives of the most massive stars), and perhaps by even more powerful events. Astronomers are still trying to determine the source of some brief—but brilliant—gamma-ray "bursts."

MIRRORS FOR EXTREMES

A major problem when trying to build high-energy telescopes is that X-rays and gamma rays tend to pass straight through mirrors—and most other things—as though they weren't there. To get around this, astronomers use some imaginative ideas. Most X-ray telescopes use a series of metal "mirrors" with curved shapes, nested inside each other. This causes the X-rays to bounce off the mirror at shallow angles, ricocheting just like a bullet. These are known as "grazing incidence" mirrors, and they are arranged so that they bring the X-rays to a focus for study just like a traditional telescope.

Gamma rays are more of a challenge because they pass through X-ray mirrors. They can be detected in "spark chambers," however. These are made from crisscrossed wires, each carrying an electric current but separated from the others in a gas-filled chamber. The incoming gamma ray allows the gas to briefly conduct electricity, so a spark jumps between two of the wires. By stacking spark chambers on top of each other and tracing the positions of the sparks as they go off in each of them, astronomers can determine the path and direction of the original gamma ray. The main Gamma-ray telescope currently in orbit is the European Space Agency's *INTErnational Gamma-Ray Astrophysics Laboratory* (*INTEGRAL*).

Infrared observatories have revolutionized our view of the universe by revealing objects such as dust clouds, faint stars, and "brown dwarfs" (failed stars), which are too faint and cool to shine in visible light. The challenge for anyone building an infrared telescope is to keep it cool. Temperatures in orbit can vary from -185 to 250 °Fahrenheit (-120 to 121 °Celsius) in a matter of minutes. An infrared telescope must be constantly chilled in order to prevent its own heat from swamping the radiation from distant stars. For this reason, infrared telescopes are usually enclosed in an insulating jacket that acts like a thermos. Inside this jacket, coolants such as liquid helium keep the telescope at temperatures as low as –450 °F (–270 °C). The coolant eventually leaks away, so most infrared telescopes only operate for a few years.

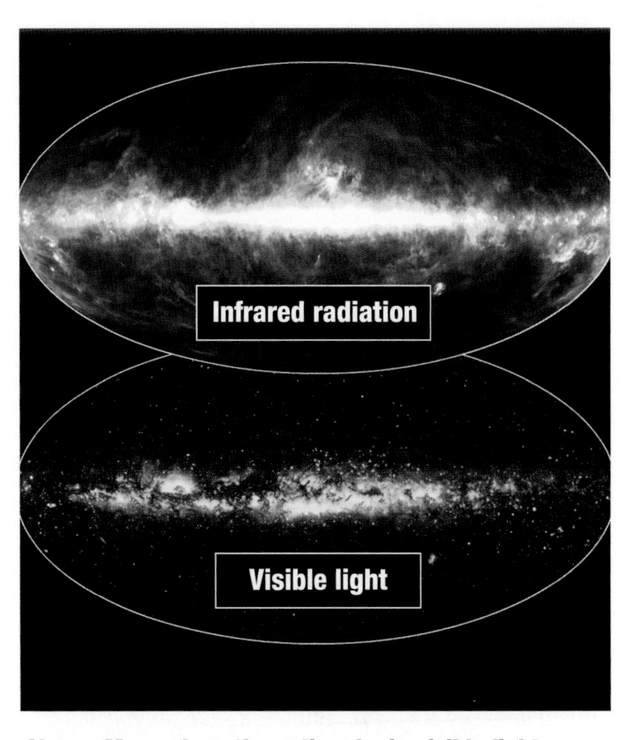

Above: Maps show the entire sky in visible light (lower), and in infrared (upper) radiation. The bright band of the Milky Way stands out clearly in both pictures.

Below: An artist's conception of NASA's *Chandra* X-ray Observatory, with NGC 604 in the background. Deployed by the space shuttle *Columbia* in 1999, it is the most sophisticated X-ray observatory yet built.

GLOSSARY

aperture: an opening or open space such as a hole; the aperture lets light into a telescope or camera.

asteroid: a rocky body smaller than a moon that orbits a star. Asteroids vary in size from a few yards across to hundreds of miles wide.

asterism: a certain set of the entire group of stars that makes up a constellation.

concave: hollowed or rounded inward.

constellation: a group of stars that, from Earth, forms a recognizable pattern on the night sky. Constellations are usually named after people, places, or objects from mythology, but some are named after scientific instruments or animals.

convex: curved or rounded outward.

distort: to twist out of shape from the original.

gyroscope: an instrument consisting of a spinning wheel or disk mounted on an axle in such a way that it always points in the same direction no matter how it is tilted.

infrared (IR): invisible form of radiation emitted by hot and warm objects; also called heat radiation.

interferometry: the combined measurement of the interaction of two or more wavelengths of light, radiation, sound, or other type of wavelength; often used to refer to the practice of using a number of telescopes spaced widely apart in order to increase the overall viewing area.

Middle Ages: a period of European history that lasted from about A.D. 500 to 1450.

parabola: a curved shape that reflects all light or signals to a point of focus on its surface.

planetarium: a special dome-shaped theater in which a simulated picture or animation of the night sky is projected onto the ceiling.

prism: a transparent body, usually glass, with a somewhat triangular shape; its purpose is to bend, or refract, visible light rays and split them into their component colors.

reflect: to change direction of light or sound waves, causing them to "bounce" back toward their origin or toward another direction.

refraction: the deflection, or bending, of energy waves caused when the speed at which the waves, such as electromagnetic radiation or visible light rays, are traveling changes; usually caused when the energy waves pass from one medium, such as air, into another, such as glass.

resolve (for telescopes): to clarify fine details and to separate objects in space from one another.

spectrum: an ordered arrangement that can be broken down into its many components.

ultraviolet (UV): invisible electromagnetic radiation with wavelengths shorter than visible light but longer than X-rays.

FURTHER INFORMATION

BOOKS

Dyer, Alan, et al. B*ackyard Astronomy: Your Guide to Starhopping and Exploring the Universe.* Nature Company Guides (2001).
Kerrod, Robin. Starwatch: *A Month-by-Month Guide to the Night Sky.* Barron's Educational Series (2003).
Rau, Dana Meachen. *Constellations.* Our Solar System (series). Compass Point Books (2005).
Scagell, Robin. *The Night Sky Atlas: The Moon, Planets, Stars And Deep Sky Objects.* Firefly Books (2005).
Sparrow, Giles (Ed.). *The Night Sky: Discovering the Universe from Alpha Centauri to Quasars.* Thunder Bay Press (2006).
Sparrow, Giles. *The Universe and How to See It: A Practical Guide to Viewing & Understanding the Night Sky.* Reader's Digest Books (2001).

WEB SITES

www.backyard-astro.com/beginner/beginner.html
Find out how to become an amateur astronomer.

www.xmission.com/~alanne/AstronomyBeginning.html
Read tips and get information from a hands-on amateur astronomer.

http://skyandtelescope.com/howto/basics/article_260_1.asp
Get a good start on your search for the stars.

www.space.com
Visit the best Web site for daily space news.

http://antwrp.gsfc.nasa.gov/apod/astropix.html
Check out NASA's picture of the day.

http://hubblesite.org/
See the latest from the Hubble Space Telescope.

Publisher's note to educators and parents: Our editors have carefully reviewed these Web sites to ensure that they are suitable for children. Many Web sites change frequently, however, and we cannot guarantee that a site's future contents will continue to meet our high standards of quality and educational value. Be advised that children should be closely supervised whenever they access the Internet.

INDEX

absorption lines 11
adaptive optics (AO) 41
age of the universe 13
Albireo 34
Alcor 34
Algol 37
Alpha Centauri 32–33
alt-azimuth systems 18, 21
altitudes 18
Andromeda Galaxy 15
apparent magnitudes 15
Arcturus 33
Arecibo 10–11, 42
Aristarchus 6
ascension 18
asteroids 11, 28
astrology 5
astrophysics 11–13

Bayer, Johann 32
Bessel, Friedrich 11
Beta Centauri 33
Betelgeuse 31, 33
big bang theory 13
Big Dipper 34
binary stars 34–35
binoculars 15–16, 20
black holes 13, 44
Brahe, Tycho 8
brightnesses 12, 15, 32–33
brown dwarfs 34, 45

Canopus 32
catalogs 11–12, 32
celestial spheres 18
Cetus 37
Chandra 11, 45
Charged Coupled Devices (CCDs) 19
classifications 32
clocks 10
clusters 35
colors of stars 35, 36
Columbia 45
comets 28
computers 19
conjunctions 27
constellations 31–32
coordinates 18
Copernicus, Nicolaus 6–8
cosmic background radiation 13
cosmology 13

dark energy 13
dark matter 13
declination 18
Delta Cephei 37
Deneb 33
distances 11, 35
Dobsonian mounts 21
Doppler effect 12
double stars (*see also binary stars*) 34–35

Earth 6, 23
Earthshine 24
eclipses 26–27
ecliptic 23
Eddington, Arthur 13
Einstein, Albert 13
electromagnetic spectrum 8, 10–11, 13, 42
Endeavour 23
Epsilon Lyrae 34
equatorial telescopes 21
Eta Carinae 37

expanding universe 13
extreme stars 34
eyepieces 17
eyesight 15

Flamsteed, John 32
Fraunhofer, Joseph von 11

galaxies 13
Galilei, Galileo 8, 9
gamma rays 8, 11, 42, 44
Gamov, George 13
giant telescopes 39–41
gravity 10
Great Red Spot 28
Greece 6
Gregory, James 8–10

Halley's comet 10
Harriot, Thomas 24–25
Henry Draper catalog 11–12, 32
Herschel, William 10–11, 13
Hertzsprung-Russell diagram 12
history of astronomy 5–13
Hubble, Edwin 13
Hubble Space Telescope (*HST*) 11, 23, 39, 41
Huygens, Christopher 8
Hyades 35

ice dwarfs 29
inferior planets 26
infrared (IR) 8, 10
infrared telescopes 10–11, 45
interferometry 39, 42

Jansky, Karl 42
Jewel Box 35
Jodrell Bank 43
Jupiter 9, 27–28

Keck telescopes 39–40
Kepler, Johannes 8
Kuiper Belt Objects (KBO) 29

laws of motion 10
Lemaître, Georges 13
lenses 16–17, 20, 39
light-years 13
Lovell, Bernard 42, 43
lunar eclipses 26

magnitudes 15
Mars 27
Mercury 26
microwave telescopes 11
Milky Way 45
Mira 37
mirrors 16–17, 21, 44
Mizar 34
Moon 24–25
Mount Palomar 39
M13 35

nebulae 36
Neptune 11, 28
neutron stars 34
Newton, Isaac 8–10
NGC 604 45

Omega Centauri 35
Oort Cloud 29
opposition 27
optical instruments 16–17
orbiting observatories 44–45

Orion 31, 36
outer planets 26–28

Perseus 37
photographs 19
photography 11
photometry 19
planetarium programs 19
Pleiades 35
Pluto 29
prisms 17, 20
Proxima Centauri 33
Ptolemy 6, 7, 31
pulsars 34
pyramids 5

radiation 42
radio telescopes 10–11, 42–43
Reber, Grote 42
red dwarfs 34
red giants 32–33
reflecting telescopes 8–10, 21, 39
refracting telescopes 17, 20, 39
Renaissance 6
retrograde motion 27
Rigel 31, 33
right ascension (R.A.) 18, 21
Russell, Henry Norris 12

satellites (artificial) 11
Saturn 8, 28
Sirius 15, 32
solar eclipses 26–27
space-based telescopes 10–11
Special Theory of Relativity 13
spectroscopy 11–12
speed of light 13
Spitzer, Lyman 41
Spitzer Space Telescope 11
Sputnik 11, 43
The Starry Messenger (Galilei) 9
Stonehenge 5, 6
summer solstices 23
Sun 6–8, 11, 13, 23–24
superior planets 26

telescopes 8–11
  computer-controlled 19
  giant telescopes 39–41
  mounts 21
  parts of 16–17
  radio telescopes 10–11, 42–43
  recording images 19
temples 5
Titan 8, 28
twinkling stars 40
types of stars 34

ultraviolet 8, 10, 44
umbras 27
Uranus 11, 28
UV telescopes 11

variable stars 37
Vega 33
Venus 9, 26
visible light 15, 42

white dwarfs 34
winter solstices 23

X-rays 8, 11, 42, 44

zodiacs 5